I0618471

Blood, Salt, and Soil

Tennille Nicolette

If you have a garden and a library, you have everything you need.

--Marcus Tillius Cicero

Tennille Nicolette
Blood, Salt, and Soil
ISBN: 978-0692973523
© 2017
Cover art by Julia Kolyanda
https://www.fiverr.com/julia__kolyanda

Table of Contents

Preface

This book is part catharsis, part fantasy. I hope you enjoy reading it as much as I enjoyed writing it.

Much love and thanks to my mom, who pegged me as a writer at the age of four and provided the pencils and paper.

Infinite appreciation to my husband, who gives me the space, time, and tea to focus on this and all my other 'bucket list' items.

And thank you to Nami, who knitted me a pink pussy hat. I will cherish it forever.

1

Ancient History

"It's beautiful."

On this bright winter day, in my best friend Twinkie's suburban front yard, the gang and I labored for hours to engineer a chest-high snow fort complete with windows, a guest bedroom, and a built-in cooler for soda cans. Katie just finished sculpting a snow-vase behind a front window for Maggie's silk flowers. We paused to admire their thoughtful finishing touch. My eyes soaked up the novel contrast of Maggie's pink rose petals against the crisp, white snow. In that moment, the comforting heat under my coat, the brisk chill of my cheeks, the sense of camaraderie and pride of accomplishment, all made me feel intoxicatingly alive. I recall thinking, this day I will remember.

We were too distracted by our mission to smooth out the south walls to hear footsteps approaching us. I guess it wouldn't have mattered, because it never occurred to us to build any sort of defense in case of a threat. In this quiet, suburban neighborhood, the worst threat we anticipated was the christening of our pristine snow by Mrs. Anderson's golden retriever.

So we were completely caught unprepared for the tall boy's opening salvo, a swift kick to the north wall. Maggie's flowers plunged unceremoniously into the snow. The tall boy laughed as my best friend Twinkie cried out indignantly. I didn't recognize him, but he looked to be high-school age. Maybe he was from the family that moved down the street a few months ago; if he'd always lived here, he wouldn't have come to destroy what we had built. He kicked the north wall again, collapsing our cute arched front door.

"Stop it!!" Twinkie yelled.

"Make me," the boy retorted. He stepped over to deliver a kick to the last part of our north wall.

We outnumbered him four to one, but he had the upper hand. He was more willing to destroy our snow fort than we were willing to destroy him. So we stood frozen for a moment in a dramatic stare-down.

Maggie was the first to move. She reached down to her upturned silk flowers, grabbed them, then bolted. Katie followed her, as fast as she could run. I watched them for just a moment, before I turned to look at Twinkie. Her eyes, burning with indignation, darted from Maggie's fleeing figure to me, then to the tall boy.

"You get out of here. This is my yard." She said it so resolutely, I was impressed.

"Yeah, like I care." The boy took a step closer to her, his boot penetrating the remains of our front wall. He just breached our precious snow fort. This means war.

In a desperate flash, I took off toward Twinkie's house, threw the door open and ran downstairs to the den, shamelessly violating their house rules against tracking snow into the house. Twinkie's dad was watching a football game on the couch. I breathlessly implored him to scare off the boy in the front yard, but he just looked at me and answered,

"You girls need to learn to take care of yourselves."

I ran back outside to our snow fort, now in shambles. The boy had Twinkie pinned down in the wreckage. I growled and charged the boy, knocking him off of her. I felt the shock of ice cold in my ears and sweaty hair as we tumbled into the snow.

The tall boy crawled on top of me. His gaze was pure, cold hatred. He spat on my face.

"You better not fucking touch me again."

He stood up, kicked me in my side, grabbed one of our sodas, then walked away.

I looked over at Twinkie. She was sitting up, crying. Her long brown hair stuck to the tears on her bright red cheeks.

"Are you OK, Twinkie?"

"Yeah, are you?"

"Yeah." I sat up, wiped the spit off my face with my glove, then took the glove off and wiped it off in the snow.

"Where'd you go?"

"I, uh, ran to go tell your dad."

"Oh."

Twinkie looked down her hands in her lap as we sat silently in the snow. We both knew her dad wasn't likely to leave his couch to help her with anything. I suddenly felt foolish for even trying, and sorry Twinkie would probably get teased about it at the dinner table later.

"Don't worry, we'll get back at that boy." I tried to sound optimistic.

"How? He tossed us around like rag dolls and we don't even know where he came from."

The next day, Twinkie and I were walking home from school when we saw Maggie's head in her backyard – not her body, just her auburn curls. Curious, we stepped into her yard to find she had partly recreated our snow fort, albeit a smaller, less complicated version.

"I'm sorry I ran. I was scared of that boy," she said simply.

"That's OK." I answered.

"Did you beat that bully yesterday?" She asked.

"No."

"I did." Maggie patted another handful of snow onto a wall.

"No you didn't," Twinkie said.

"But it feels like I did," Maggie answered. She stood up and beckoned us inside. Her pink silk flowers stood proudly out of a small mound of snow in the corner.

So, that's ancient history.

I realized our story needed to start there, before you read anything else. Otherwise, you might not understand why the rest of my story unfolded as it did. And we really want whoever reads this to understand, while we aren't exactly proud of everything we've done, we don't really regret any of it, either.

We call it ancient history because our past, like that afternoon playing in our snow fort, could not be relived today. That world doesn't exist anymore. Twinkie's mom and dad wouldn't be allowed to meet, let alone marry and have Twinkie. Katie's parents wouldn't have been allowed to move here, so she'd be just a stranger halfway across the world from us. (To be fair, though, her grades probably would have turned out much better.)

And our innocence, our blissful ignorance of hatred, might never grace a childhood here again. We were shocked at encountering hatred for the first time at nine years of age. Now it's everywhere; woven into daily conversation, factored into every decision, paraded on TV like it's something to be proud of. Nobody would even consider shielding a child from hatred now, because they want them to learn it. Pass it on like an old, broken pocket watch.

Last but not least, it's ancient history because we are so different than the kids we used to be. I'd always assumed that, since we had grown up together, we just knew each other, down to our bones, and always would. If we stuck together, we would remain the same, and rely on each other's consistency to sail through sunsets and bright dawns and stormy weather alike. Luckily for us, part of that turned out to be true: we have stuck together through turbulent times.

But our experiences changed us in ways our younger selves wouldn't be able to fathom. Maggie and Twinkie and Katie and I found each other doing things our kid selves wouldn't have believed possible. But it isn't that we didn't really know each other; we just didn't really know ourselves.

I'm the resident archivist, given my addiction to the written word. If I haven't collected a book that explains how to do something, I learn from someone else, then spend the time to write it down for posterity. Recently, I decided I wanted to write the why, not just the how, behind our lives, behind our decisions. The truth will be free, eventually. And when it does, here's hoping that, through this story, you've walked enough miles in our moccasins to understand and forgive us.

We grew up together in a milquetoast Midwest city that's struggled to keep up with the world since cars were invented. There was just enough opportunity to keep us there – enough jobs to go around, a couple of colleges, festivals every summer, pubs and clubs to hit on the weekends. Not enough there to make us wealthy or worldly, just enough to prevent us from dying of boredom.

So we stayed together, hanging out in nearly the same ways at 15 and 25 that we did at 5, making the best of our mediocrity with fleeting diversions and enduring friendships. Our obsessions drifted from cartoons and video games, to boy bands, to boys, and then for some of us, back to cartoons and video games. Our friend group occasionally grew or shrunk by one, but stayed more or less the same. Katie introduced us to Nicole after they met in community college; I brought in Stephanie from my school. Shelby had always been around, just with frequently divergent interests. She was the sort of kid that you never knew if she was going to show up at a gathering, but it was always more fun when she did.

Through it all, Twinkie has been the glue that's held us all together. Between you and me, I think there were three reasons for it; an insatiable desire to organize things, extraversion, and annoyingly strict parents. She got her nickname when she became obsessed with Twinkies in the third grade. (Her real name is Aaliyah.) Her family wouldn't buy those "haram things," (they're not haram, actually - I checked) but she loved them. As soon as she realized she could trade for Twinkies at school, she launched an impressive operation of networking and bartering that ultimately netted her at least one Twinkie per day. At the lunch table, she'd hold up whatever goodie she'd managed to snag through pre-lunch negotiations, until a taker waved a baggie of the yellow snack cake and called out, "Twinkie!" It quickly became the most effective way to get her attention, so the name stuck.

I slowly grew more timid over the years, but Twinkie never did. For a long time, the moment I tackled the bully seemed like the last moment I had any courage. We never really talked about it, but in hindsight, I think that day cemented Twinkie's resolve to be herself and make things happen no matter what the obstacles were.

Have you ever heard of the boiling frog? It's said that if you drop a frog into a pot of boiling water, it will jump out to save itself; if you drop it in cold water then slowly boil it, the frog won't notice the heat until it's too late, and cooks to death. I think it's possible that if Twinkie hadn't been dropped in the boiling water first, none of us would have escaped our increasingly hotter pot. And perhaps Twinkie would have been the only one able to pull us all out before it was too late.

2

Bite Me, Kitchen Club Emporium

"Ex-cuse me?!" I heard Twinkie raise her voice before I saw what was happening. She doesn't say it that way unless she's about to go ballistic.

I headed straight toward the sound of her voice, around the aisle, past the pyramid display of cookware sets and up to a potbellied security guard watching Twinkie, who was obviously flustered by the store employee in front of her. The security guard stuck out his arm to stop me from approaching her.

"You have no right to ask me to leave," Twinkie exclaimed. "I want to talk to your manager."

"I am the manager. And I'm not asking you to leave, I'm telling you. Please do so now before I call the police."

"Twinkie, what's going on?" I said, alarmed. I've known Twinkie practically my whole life. She's never gotten into trouble anywhere, and valued her spotless reputation. I've even seen her give up on friendships with troublemakers just to keep her nose clean.

"They're kicking me out! Just like that! I haven't done anything!"

"Hello, excuse me?" I stepped around the security guard and toward the manager. "There must be some mistake," I cooed, giving him my best 'I'm a good citizen' smile.

"This is not your concern," the manager said patronizingly. The security guard stepped forward to stand beside me.

"Yeah it is, she's my friend."

"Then please escort her out. She's behaving inappropriately."

I looked around to see if a crowd was forming. A couple of women nearby discreetly turned their heads back to the merchandise to pretend they weren't watching.

"You're the ones behaving inappropriately," I retorted, raising my voice in frustration. "You have no right to make her leave if she's not doing anything wrong!"

It seemed like a ripe case of racial profiling. I don't care if it is legal now, that is completely unacceptable to me.

"I'm sorry but we do have the right to dismiss anyone. Company policy. Officer, will you please show them out?" The manager backed up as the security guard stepped toward Twinkie.

"Your bosses are going to hear about this," Twinkie retorted, and turned away to leave. I followed her out of the store.

"So what happened?" I asked as I caught up to her.

"Nothing! I was standing in front of the buffet servers and that bitch just walked to up to me and told me to leave."

"That's it? No reason? Did she accuse you of shoplifting?"

"Oh! Well first she said, 'we're putting in new measures to increase the safety and comfort of our customers,' and I said, 'Oh, that's nice,' and then she said, 'so we need you to leave.'"

"But you're in there all the time. You're probably one of their best customers." That was true. She hit that store like other people hit gas stations or grocery stores.

"Well, NOT ANYMORE! OH! I'm so pissed!"

It was still chilly enough on this early spring day, I could see her breath; it looked as angry as she sounded, like a fire-breathing dragon getting ready to blow. She slid into the passenger seat of my car and slammed the door shut. My mind ran through our options. What can make this situation better? Call the police? Call the local TV station? Ram my car through their front window?

(The most aggravating thing to me is, not only is she a natural born citizen, you can't even tell where her ancestors are from. People have guessed she was Indian, Native American, and Hispanic, or just really tan for a white person. In the past, whenever a bigot would call her a racial slur, she'd tell them they guessed wrong. Usually they'd give up and leave her alone. Truth is, she's half Iranian, which is not something you openly admit these days. So she calls herself Persian, because most Americans don't know it's the same place.)

I sat for a moment with my phone, trying in vain to find the corporate contact number for the Kitchen Club Emporium, ready to give them a piece of my mind. But their website offered no means to contact them. It was just an advertisement. I cast about for something to salvage our afternoon. Maybe something tried and true… but she's way too angry right now to be drinking martinis.

"Hey, I know what'll cheer you up," I said, trying to sound chipper.

"I don't want to be cheered up right now. I feel sick, I'm so angry."

"Trust me."

We drove to our favorite mani-pedi place down the street and settled in to a session. Twinkie asked for a slip of paper to write down her order; otherwise, she was serious-face and silent. I felt bad for her, and mad too. The Kitchen Club Emporium was her favorite place. She spent so much time and money in there these last three years, her own kitchen looked like a page on their website. But now she's not welcome there. It's just not right.

I broke from my reverie to gaze at the women working on our nails. Usually they're chatty with each other in a language I don't understand. Today they're quiet and look tense. I cleared my throat.

"Hello, how are you today?" I asked kindly.

"I'm fine, how are you," she replied politely.

"You look sad. Is everything OK?"

My manicure lady sighed. "My shop shut down, this our last week. My husband not allowed to come back into the country, so we go to him."

"I'm sorry," I respond sadly, sincerely.

The manicure lady resumed her work. I looked down at my nails. This is my favorite color, a pretty rosy pink. But there's no pleasure in this experience; we're all just kind of going through the motions. We were doing everything normally, but the world seemed different. They finished our nails. We tipped them extra and gave them hugs goodbye.

I don't know what was the final straw for Twinkie, but for me, it was the horror we witnessed on the drive home that day.

We were driving on the interstate on the way back to Twinkie's house. Suddenly, traffic slowed to a creep in response to flashing police lights by the right side of the road. Twinkie cursed rubberneckers as per usual. As we approached the scene, I could see two police cars parked in the shoulder on either end of a pickup truck and a small sedan, neither of which looked like they'd been in an accident. My car melted into the mass of passerby vehicles with a front row view of what was happening by the side of the road.

"Oh my god," Twinkie said quietly.

Two beefy white guys were beating and kicking a smaller black man crumpled up on the road next to the sedan. Two police officers stood next to the men. One was just standing still, with his arms crossed. The other officer was pointing his gun at the man getting beaten. As we passed them, I heard somebody yell, "get up, I dare you!"

"Stop the car!" Twinkie yelled at me suddenly.

"And do what?" I yelped back. "Get our asses kicked? Get arrested? What would that accomplish?"

Twinkie turned away from me silently.

"Why are they even doing that?!" I exclaimed angrily.

Twinkie glanced at me with a dark look.

"Why do you think?"

Caught in the tide of rubberneckers, we helplessly drifted past them. The car was moving, but it felt like time itself had stood still.

Still looking away, Twinkie asked, "there was a woman in the passenger seat of that dude's car, did you see her?"

"No."

"I wonder what's gonna happen to her."

"I don't know…."

The sea of cars ahead of us spread out and sped up; the space between our car and theirs steadily grew. I found myself wondering where we should really drive from here.

Finally, Twinkie broke the silence.

"Hey." She looked at me with her sly smile. "I have a plan."

She always does. That's one of the reasons why she's my bestie.

"Okay. But I need a drink first," I sighed. I'd seen way too much social injustice for one afternoon, and it wasn't even happening to me.

I watched Twinkie make a couple of lemon drop martinis for us in her kitchen, prepared in a Kitchen Club Emporium brushed stainless shaker and served in Kitchen Club Emporium glasses. Couldn't help but notice the blank space on her counter where the buffet server was supposed to go, if the Kitchen Club Emporium had actually let her buy it today. I also couldn't help but notice that Twinkie is in a decidedly better mood, more like the woman I'm familiar with. As she handed me a glass, I finally noticed her manicure. Tiny letters stenciled onto her fingernails spelled out "fuck you." Wow, I thought, she must be feeling ornery!

"You know what I want?" She sat down in front of me.

"A buffet server?"

"No."

"The Kitchen Club Emporium manager's job?"

Twinkie rolled her eyes and smiled. "I just want peace and freedom for myself and my friends. No matter if it's hard to do."

"Me too."

"So let's do something about it." She started shaking the drink shaker rhythmically.

"Like what?"

"Let's just… stop. Stop participating. Stop reading the news and watching this train wreck slowly unfold. Let's just go, get out of here." She stopped shaking, the sudden quiet punctuating her call to action.

"What are you talking about?" I asked.

"I mean like, leave this craziness, get back to the basics. Hide away together, grow our own food, build our own shelter. Just *live* for a while, cut out all the bullshit." Twinkie uncapped the shaker, then poured our martinis.

"That's crazy."

"No it's not." She handed me my glass.

"It sounds kinda crazy."

"It's how more than half the world lives, every day. Why is that crazy?"

"That's a good point." I looked away to think for a minute. "But I don't know how to do all that stuff."

"Neither do I, but we can find out how. People used to live that way all the time. Plus, we have tons of modern tools and stuff, like toilet paper and marshmallow vodka and silicone handled spatulas."

"Hey I have silicone handled things, they're amazing."

"Yes they are. We'll take 'em with us. We'll have it so much easier than the pioneers or whoever. We'll make it look good."

We sipped our martinis for a minute in silence.

"You're serious…?"

"Yeah, I am."

"Build our own shelter?" I asked. "Wouldn't it be easier to just rent one?"

"Yeah," Twinkie admitted. "Maybe a cool cabin out in the woods, like the kind my family rents in the Smokies for big family reunions."

"That actually sounds awesome. Let's go look for something!" I grinned at her.

Twinkie jumped up and quickly returned with her laptop to her kitchen table. I sat down beside her to watch over her shoulder as she browsed the internet.

"I'm imagining it would be like glamping," said Twinkie, "and I've always wanted to go glamping." (Glamping = glamorous camping, for anyone who doesn't watch as much TV as Twinkie.)

We sipped our drinks as she pulled up rustic cabin rentals within 100 miles of home.

"That one is way too small."

"That one looks like the site of a grisly ax murder."

"I know, right?!"

"Wow, what about that one! It's so cute!"

"Yeah, but it's $200 a night."

"OUCH. Never mind. What about the smaller one?"

"Let's see…. Nope. It's already booked through the summer."

There were more options 200 miles from home, but that seemed too far away.

"Well, how long were you thinking of being gone?" I asked her, sipping my martini, licking the tang off my upper lip. "Maybe $200 a night wouldn't be so bad, if we split it."

"Months? Maybe longer?" She asked slowly, watching my reaction. My eyebrows flew up as I stared back at her, wondering what was going on in her head. She was dead serious, that much was obvious. After knowing her so long, I could read her like a book.

"Wow. You really are talking about checking out."

"Yeah. I feel sucked into a rigged rat race I can never win. And I'm just tired of it. Aren't you?"

I fell silent. I know I'm not as invested in the world as other people I know. I don't keep up with pop culture or fashion trends or what's the newest thing streaming, but it would feel strange leaving it all behind.

"Yeah, but it seems so drastic," I finally answered, looking into her eyes.

"It's not really. It's not like we'd be moving to a foreign country, learning a new language, converting all our money, giving up our citizenship."

"That's true," I conceded.

"We could fade back in as easily as we fade out. We can just try it, and see if we like it." She raised her martini glass and took a sip.

"Well, there's no way we could afford fading out at $200 a night."

Twinkie sighed and closed her laptop. "Well... I'm not giving up yet. Hey. Wait a minute. What about my uncle's house?"

"You want to move in with your uncle?"

"No, no. He has about 35 acres of wooded property a few miles outside town with several outbuildings. Maybe he'd let us stay in one of them."

"Are any of them like houses?" I asked.

"No, but at least they're buildings, already standing. We could just fix one up."

"Like, with electricity?"

"Yeah, I can find out," she replied, smiling.

"I guess, as long as it doesn't smell like horse butts, something like that might work," I said.

"I'm going to find out!" She pulled out her phone to call her aunt and uncle. A moment later, she had an appointment to visit their property the next day. Her uncle, Jack, said he had an old pole barn he could let us use.

"You know, maybe we should invite a few others," she suggested.

"Who are you thinking?" I asked.

"Like Katie. Her parents died a while ago."

"Yeah. Oh man, she's so good with crafts, she can probably build anything. I think she even does carpentry and stuff."

"Yeah. Or Nicole. Her parents moved to China."

"I didn't know that."

"And Maggie. You know she has a ton of food at her house."

"Oh, Twinkie. This sounds like it could be fun, but let's be realistic. We have rent to pay, we have jobs, we can't just walk away from all of that."

"Why not?" she said simply.

I opened my mouth to give some reasons, but couldn't think of any.

"All that stuff will be here when we come back. And really. What of any of that stuff do you actually NEED to live? What would your landlord do if you don't finish your leases, throw you in jail? No. They can't really do anything. That's why assholes get away with skipping leases all the time. We can all be assholes for once in our lives."

"I guess that's true," I agreed.

"And when we're ready to come back, we just pick up jobs again. You guys can stay with me until you get back on your feet." Knowing Twinkie as well as I do, I believed her.

"Yeah, that would work," I replied. "Your house will stay yours…. But why not just stay here? We can unplug here just as easily."

"I don't want to do that. It wouldn't be *different* enough. I want escape… not a giant, nonstop sleepover at my house. I want to be gone." She shook her head.

"Fair enough," I nodded.

"If we go out to the country, we'd be living like survivors in *The Walking Dead*, without the zombies," she said, grinning.

"I love that show!"

"Or the *Boxcar Children*. Without the zombies."

"Ha ha! I loved those books."

"Me too."

She refilled our glasses, then raised hers up to toast.

"To taking a break from bullshit."

Clink.

3

Fight or Flight, Party Edition

Twinkie's visit with her aunt Janet and uncle Jack went extraordinarily well, it seemed to me from her recounting later over text. Her family sounded like really nice people, just like Twinkie. When she told them about her crazy idea, they offered to let us use an old wooden pole barn and the surrounding land without much hesitation. Twinkie suspected they liked the idea that someone else in their family would get back to their roots, emulating their rural lifestyle.

Apparently, Jack had been using that pole barn for equipment storage until last fall, when he decided he needed more space. He had a bigger barn built closer to his house, and just finished moving most of his equipment into the new building. So the pole barn was still intact, still had electricity, and never stored livestock. Twinkie toured it and pronounced it "super cute" and "totally perfect for us." That was good enough for me.

Once Twinkie had a location for our adventure worked out, it was time to petition the others to join her. I automatically agreed, because that's how we operate. She makes the plans, and I follow them. Maggie's always been our best friend too, but we weren't sure she would come with us. Same with the others. So in typical Twinkie style, she decided to throw a party to spring the idea on them all.

"Hey!" I called as I let myself in. I could hear my friends chatting in the kitchen over Django Reinhart as I kicked off my shoes and hung up my jacket.

Twinkie met me at the door, her eyes twinkling. She leaned in for a hug.

"Oh you should see what I bought for us! I can't wait to show you."

"Sweet!"

"Yeah. We're still waiting on Katie and Nicole. Come grab a drink!"

I followed her in to see our usual gang gathered around the well-appointed snack tray on the kitchen table, as is typical for Twinkie's parties. Stephanie is here, I'm glad; she doesn't always take us up on invitations, but of my semi-best friends, she'd definitely be someone I'd want on my side in a zombie apocalypse, pretend or otherwise.

Shelby was there too, standing with Maggie and her sister Breanna. It's interesting seeing Maggie and Breanna stand together because of their drastic difference in styles, knowing they're related. Maggie is tall and pale, with shoulder length auburn hair and warm brown eyes. She's slightly heavier (and healthier looking) than her bottle-blonde, tanaholic younger sister, who looks like a *Sorority Vixens* model but with pants on. Honestly, they don't have very much in common, but since Breanna's boyfriend had recently broken up with her to join the Army, Breanna had to move in with Maggie. She couldn't afford a place on her own.

Someone tapped my shoulder – Katie – and gave me a hug. Nicole was smiling behind her.

"Hey, sorry I still haven't delivered your Christmas present yet," Katie said to me. "I've been super busy. Phone canvassing for the next big sit-in."

"What are those?" Shelby pointed toward Nicole's contribution to the snack table.

"Chia crunchies with pomegranate and pumpkin seed."

Shelby wrinkled her nose. "Why are they brown?"

"They're covered in chocolate."

Shelby's skepticism disappeared instantly. "All right!" She grabbed one and nommed it. "Guub, fank you!" she said through her mouthful.

Nicole smiled. "You're welcome. Where's the bottle opener?"

While we all sat together in the living room and chatted, I noticed how similar we all look from when we were kids (except for Stephanie, who I met in college). For the most part, we're all just bigger versions of our kid selves, outside and in.

Twinkie is still the shortest, voluptuous since early middle school, with striking green eyes to offset her beautiful light cocoa skin. She seems to have an infinite energy for gathering and entertaining people. Social gatherings that would take me days to plan and stress me out, she does effortlessly a few times a week. She's done it to keep our old neighborhood group together all this time, even though we've all spread out across the city and developed different interests.

Shelby has always had a sweet angel face, big brown eyes, full lips and doll-like, straight blonde hair, which always helped her get attention from grown-ups when we were kids, attention from the boys in school, and attention from whomever she wants now. She always knows how to dress for the occasion, always knows where the best food is, and always keeps a spare pair of panties in her purse. She's one of those larger-than-life people, the kind introverts like me can only marvel at. Always hopping from one social gathering to another, she dances, runs 5Ks, does charity work, that sort of thing. She dates multiple people at once too, but never seems to get heartbroken. And she always looks perfect and happy. I don't know how she does it.

Katie and Nicole have changed the most over the years though. Katie has always worn stylish clothes, but now that her uptight parents aren't around to shame her out of it, she's converted to an edgier, modern haircut, usually colored purple or blue. She seems to live and breathe creativity and art, much more now since her parents passed away.

Nicole is still our 'Nordic spaz monkey,' as Stephanie likes to call her. She used to be a lot more hyperactive, but then she discovered yoga, and that calmed her down (relatively speaking… at any given moment, she may launch into a pose). Her passion for yoga led to her teaching it at a studio, the first job she's been able to keep longer than six months. That and her high energy led to her delving deeply into the world of organic foods and the vegan lifestyle. It all seems exotic to the rest of us, but since her family was so much wealthier than ours, we're accustomed to her having and doing different, exotic things.

In a way, I'm kind of the opposite of everybody. I'm not rich, or pretty, or awesome, or creative, or gregarious. I mostly just read. I learn things and know things, most of which aren't useful, except on Trivia Night.

Finally, with everyone settled, with the chit-chat out of our systems and snacking down to a trickle, Twinkie brought up why we were all there – to discuss checking out on this grand scale.

"You serious?" asked Katie.

"I keep hearing that…." She answered.

"Yes she is." I replied with a nod.

"I did *not* have you ladies pegged as Doomsday preppers," remarked Stephanie dryly with a raised eyebrow.

"What?" Twinkie asked, perplexed.

"No, no," I replied. "We're not waiting for the Apocalypse or the Rapture. We're just taking an extended vacation."

"I got permission from my uncle for us to use his property. It's huge, 35 acres, about 15 minutes out of town. He said we can use his pole barn and do whatever we want to the land around it."

"What's a pole barn?" Shelby asked.

"It's, you know, a barn. With poles in it to hold up the roof."

"I can teach you guys pole yoga!" exclaimed Nicole happily.

"How about pole dancing?" asked Breanna.

"Gotcha covered," answered Shelby.

"We'd be out in the wild?" asked Breanna.

"I wouldn't exactly call 15 minutes out of town on private property the wild," answered Twinkie.

"Aren't there, like, wolves out there?"

"No, but they do have lots of deer."

"Do deer attack people?"

"Only if you piss them off. They hate puns," deadpanned Stephanie as she sipped her beer.

"They're scared of people, unless you're super calm and quiet," explained Twinkie. "You know, like rabbits."

"I like bunnies," said Maggie.

"But what would we eat out there?" asked Breanna.

"The bunnies," Stephanie answered matter-of-factly.

"Oh, stop, Steph," Twinkie chuckled. "We'd cook food like normal," answered Twinkie. "Maggie and I have been talking about setting up our stash. She already has six months' worth of food socked away, enough for all of us."

"I just love Costco! It's my favorite store!" sang Maggie.

"No kidding!" I laughed. She didn't get the nickname Magpie for nothing.

"We'd need more than that," said Stephanie.

"We can set up a garden near the pole barn. I found a cool book that shows how to grow a lot of food in a small space pretty easily in raised beds," I explained.

Nicole smiled. "Hey, I know a lot about organic gardening too."

"Wait a minute. How long are you talking about being out there?" asked Breanna.

"I don't know," answered Twinkie. "We don't really have to set a firm stopping point. Just however long we would rather be out there, than here."

"So, we stay out in the woods until things get better?"

"Nicer?"

"Until people start calming the fuck down."

"Will they?"

"Sure they will. They always do," I said optimistically with a shrug that accidentally betrayed my skepticism.

"Things feel weird anymore," said Maggie sadly, poking her drink with her straw. "Reading the news every day makes me feel awful. And I never felt afraid of strangers in public before. Now I'm constantly wondering which of them are trolls, or armed militia men looking for a fight, or worse."

"Every day, I think things can't get any more bizarre or backwards, but then I'm proved wrong. I'm worn out just trying to process all the different ways our Wise and Powerful Leaders keep making life worse for the rest of us on a daily basis." I said this sadly, jamming my straw through the ice in my glass in frustration.

Stephanie spoke up. "We're just caught in one colossal political and economic pussy-grab. The pendulum is swinging backwards. This sort of thing happens all over the world, all throughout history, but we thought we were too good for it to happen here, so it snuck up on us. I tell you what though… my pussy is not up for grabs."

"So we've heard," interjected Shelby dismissively.

"I hate feeling like I can't do anything about it. Makes me feel like throwing up sometimes," added Nicole.

"I am trying to do things about it," spoke up Katie, "But it doesn't seem to be working. I call, and get a full voicemail box. We go to our rep's office, they don't even show up. We deliver a petition, their assistants throw it in the shredder. I write an email, and get an automated response telling me they're gonna maintain status quo no matter what their constituents want, and they're proud of it. Proud of it! And lately, we don't even get media coverage."

"So this is a way to do something about it," Twinkie argued. "Quit participating in it like it's okay. Quit paying taxes, because it's funding all this bullshit. Quit giving them our personal information so they can keep tabs on us. Fuck 'em. Let's disengage. I mean, realistically, none of us are going to leave the country. We have nowhere else to go. We don't know any other languages."

"I thought you took Spanish," I said.

"Yeah, but all the Spanish I remember besides "please" and "thank you" is the word for paper clip," Twinkie replied.

I laughed. "That's kinda pathetic, Twinkie. But I can't do better... all I can remember from a year of Latin class is the word for 'cocksucker.'"

"Nice!" She laughed.

"I agree! And do not want to subject the lovely people of South America to my terrible Spanish."

"So if we stay, we'll at least be able to talk to the natives," Twinkie said.

"There's definitely an advantage to that. I already know the word for 'cocksucker' here," Stephanie added.

We all sat for a moment thoughtfully poking at our snack plates. I remember wondering if this was too crazy to work. Could we all really last more than two days without civilization, even as screwed up as it is these days?

Stephanie piped up. "Ladies... we're talking about walking away from everything. Like modern conveniences. We can't take them all with us. Wouldn't we end up spending all day doing things like hand-washing our underwear, and peeling potatoes and stuff like that?"

"Don't you already do those things?" Twinkie asked, looking at her funny.

"No, I'm lazy. I just throw it all in the washing machine."

"You put potatoes in the washing machine?"

Steph rolled her eyes. "Yes. In with my panties. No I'm serious, ladies. No air conditioning. No dishwashers. No cable TV... Maggie." She looked pointedly at her.

"I'm sick of cable TV," I said. Nicole and Katie agreed.

"I freaking love my TV," Maggie said. Shelby and Twinkie nodded, but Twinkie was already prepared to answer for that.

"I was gonna keep my DVR to record our favorite shows," Twinkie explained. "We can run back to my house once a week to binge watch."

"Ooh, that sounds good," Maggie replied with a smile of relief.

"Well," Stephanie interjected, "now that the important stuff is worked out... What about your jobs?"

Silence.

"Do we still go to work?" asked Maggie.

"Do we quit our jobs?" asked Katie.

"Do you like your job?" asked Stephanie.

"No...." answered almost everyone in unison. We all chuckled.

Shelby said, "It's one of my life goals to not have a job. Why do you think I date older guys?"

"Oh, is that why? We just thought you had a thing for droopy testicles," Steph said plainly.

"Ew! No!" Shelby drew back in disgust.

Twinkie said, "I hate my job. It's the same dead-end gig I took to put me through college. Still haven't found a job for my degree, and I graduated two years ago!"

"Yeah," Katie said. "I could get a new crappy job as easily as the crappy job I have now."

"Me too," said Maggie.

"What about you, Steph?" asked Twinkie.

"I haven't hardly gotten any work lately. Nobody wants to hire me anymore. One asshole last week told me I should get married and have a baby. Another said I should quit taking work away from men. And another idiot saw the "COEXIST" sticker on my car and said he wouldn't hire a socialist. I was like, 'well excuse me for wanting to co-exist.'"

"Jeez."

Nicole chimed in, "I don't want to quit my work at the studio, and I like my apartment. But I do want to hang out with you guys and I would LOVE to do some organic gardening for you!"

"You don't have to quit your job, but as long as you can contribute your fair share of labor and food and whatnot, you won't really need a job," Twinkie explained. "Together, we have enough resources to cover our necessities for a while."

After another moment of group contemplation, Maggie spoke up.

"Would we have electricity out there?"

"Yeah," I answered. "Her uncle has electricity out in the pole barn. And I'll get a backup generator just in case."

"What about internet. Wi-fi?"

"No wi-fi. Cell service is out there, but it's kinda spotty. And you'd need to keep paying for data to use it."

"Uh," several of them hemmed about the idea of living without wi-fi.

"That's part of the point," Twinkie reminded them. "We're trying to live less cluttered, focus more on real priorities."

The skeptics kind of half nodded in concession.

"I'd still miss my shows," said Maggie pensively.

"I'd miss the hot fudge custard sundaes at Benji's," said Katie.

"I'm not living without my face minerals," said Breanna.

"We can always drive into town for those things," I reminded them. "But you know what I'm not going to miss? Fake news. Clickbait. Racist, sexist assholes. Wondering if nobody swipes left on my profile because my selfie isn't sexy enough. And most of all, wondering if, when Twinkie or Katie don't text me back right away, it's because she was picked up for false charges, or worse."

"Yeah... fuck that shit." Stephanie said, draining her glass.

We continued talking, laughing, and planning our Glampathon for another hour or so. Finally, everyone else said good night. I stayed behind as usual to help Twinkie tidy up afterward.

"So, Twinkie, how do you think it went?" I asked as I grabbed a dish towel to dry the serving dishes she was washing.

"Pretty awesome, actually. I half expected the idea to be killed before the second round of cocktails, but they're really into it."

"Yeah, we don't normally have such serious conversations, I wasn't sure how that would play out."

"Me neither."

"Hey, uh, what do you think of Breanna joining us?" I asked, trying to sound casual.

"I texted Maggie about that earlier. Maggie wants to come with us, but she won't do it unless her sister and her cat can come with her."

"Ah, I forgot about the cat."

"Yeah. And Breanna doesn't have anyone else to stay with if Maggie moves out."

"That makes sense. I just feel a bit nervous about Breanna coming with us," I admitted. "We never hung out together when we were kids, and now she seems so different than the rest of us."

"Yeah, but she's still practically family. Maggie is our family, and Maggie doesn't come without her posse. Including the cat."

"Yeah. I get it. Well, I hope it works out," but the skepticism crept out through my voice.

"Don't worry," said Twinkie with a soothing confidence. "Everybody gets along at my house."

4

We Need a What?

So, the next few weeks, we planned and shopped and texted each other almost constantly in our new Glampathon private message group. We made a supply list, and divided up the prep work. Maggie of course knew where all the good sales were, and Katie found some good coupons. I busied myself collecting how-to books for gardening and food storage. Stephanie made fun of me for offering to bring books to the Glampathon, but I reminded her that we don't want to be dependent on electricity and unreliable internet service to do everything out there. Besides, there was a growing, tacit agreement that one of this project's goals was to tune out most of the outside world, and we can't really do that with our eyes glued to our phones.

Maggie, Breanna, and Stephanie decided to join Twinkie and me on the Glampathon. Maggie's participation was a sure thing, because she always goes along with Twinkie's plans (like me). I was actually surprised Stephanie agreed to join us, because she is just as much of an introvert as me, but she said she looked forward to the peace and quiet this experiment would provide.

Shelby declined except to visit us once in a while, "to see if you guys are still alive." Katie and Nicole decided they didn't want to make a clean break from everything, but liked the project enough to volunteer to help us set up, and hang out with us on weekends sometimes.

Their participation meant a lot to our group, even if they weren't going to live with us. Twinkie and I had been thinking we wouldn't be able to pull this crazy project off without their help. Katie can make anything from wood, glass, fiberglass, paper, clay, fabric, you name it. For example, she purchased canvas tarp that we could affix to the poles to make privacy partitions, and said she'd help us install and decorate them. I asked her to paint a pink lotus flower and bamboo shoots on my walls.

Nicole had planted and maintained a successful organic garden for a few years in her parents' old back yard. We'd need those skills on tap if we were going to make it longer than a few weeks, and besides, herb and flower gardens would add a lot in terms of ambience, beauty, and style. I have books about a few things, but they could never replace Katie and Nicole.

The more we texted and planned and shopped, the more confident we became that this crazy adventure would become a successful reality. We got so much cool stuff! A solar powered phone charger, a nice set of campfire tools, an electric hotplate, speckled blue enamel pots and a big dutch oven, a cast iron skillet, the aforementioned marshmallow vodka. I think we were all relieved to know the pole barn had electricity run out to it. Twinkie prepaid a year's worth of our electricity to Jack so we wouldn't burden him with extra expense.

Maggie contributed a mind-boggling amount of food and supplies. Her bulk warehouse memberships and general lack of shopping restraint served us well in getting settled. Technically she bought most of it before the idea was hatched. In a way, we were probably doing her a favor by using it all up. She was running out of room to store it all in her pantry and garage.

Maggie wasn't just contributing food; she had a chest freezer in her garage (pre-filled with heat-and-eat food), tons of white LED Christmas lights, and bulk boxes of Shabbat candles for cozy little lights in our canvas rooms at night. She already has an assortment of pretty glass candle holders, and is bringing those too.

My days were soon transformed by a haze of daydreaming overlaying whatever I was doing in real life. Like sharing cocktails with my friends before a miraculous sunset, offering a toast to the emerging starlight, saying a cheerful good night, then drawing open my canvas door to reveal a rustic, cozy, candlelit bedroom with a peaceful mural, fresh flowers, a bowl of chocolates, and a stack of books to read. I fall asleep to the sound of my besties' gentle breathing and the sound of katydids. This ongoing reverie made my real life feel tedious and irrelevant by comparison.

We set a hard date for moving into the pole barn a month from the first discussion party, but most of us individually drove out to the property a few times to measure the pole barn and future vegetable garden, bring in supplies, or just to look at it for a while. It was so pretty and peaceful out there, the more often I went there, the more eager I was to move in.

The first time I saw it, it was early evening after work. I drove a load of supplies to drop off. The scene was picture-postcard perfect. The pole barn was a big, wooden, red, classic sort of barn, with a large front door for tractors, a regular door at the side near the front, and a large square door near the top for the hayloft. I opened the side door and peered in. It was too dark to see, so I opened the door wide to let in the sunlight. Within that streak of light I let in, I could see the barn was empty. Very little light showed through cracks in the walls, which suggested we'd be pretty well protected from the elements. Along the left wall was a long plywood countertop with shelves above and beneath it, fashioned like a workshop. I looked up to see rafters; the front half of the barn had a second story for extra storage, and a pull-down ladder to access it.

The barn was nestled within much taller pine and freshly sprouted deciduous trees. The setting sun was backlighting the barn, giving the forest greenery behind it a magnificent glow, dappling the forest floor. A small, well-worn trail led from a small side door to a water pump; a larger trail (presumably the rest of Jack's driveway) began at the large front barn doors, and disappeared into the forest.

I followed the larger trail on foot, which led right to Jack's old white farmhouse and new pole barn. The barn's big front door was open; a man standing just inside it saw me and walked out to greet me. He was taller than me, but not as tall as Maggie. He looked accustomed to being tan, dingy and sweaty, but remembered to wipe his face and hands with a classic red handkerchief as he approached me.

"Jack?" I called out.

"That's me."

"Good evening, sir. My name is Emily. I'm one of Twi- I mean Aaliyah's friends." I reached out to shake his hand. It was warm, tough as old leather, dirt ground into the wrinkles like it had always been there.

"You girls out here to look at the pole barn?"

"Yes sir, but I'm by myself. It's my first time out here. I saw the path and wanted to see where it led."

"Yep. That was my original barn. I like my new one though. It's closer to the house, and a fair amount bigger."

"Your new building looks really nice," I added. The new pole barn was an aluminum-sided kit barn on a smooth cement foundation. It was cleaner and sleeker and much larger, but I thought to myself the older wooden barn was a lot more charming.

"I'm afraid y'all can't use the new one. It's for my equipment."

"Oh, that's okay, we would prefer the old wooden one anyway. It's perfect."

"I like things pretty quiet around here. Y'all aint gonna be throwing wild parties out here, are you?"

"No sir, we'll be quiet."

"Well, that's what Aaliyah said. I told her y'all could come out here because she's family. She said y'all are pretty close."

"Yes sir, we're like family to each other."

Jack grunted in acceptance. He pulled a cigarette out of the pack in his shirt pocket and lit it with an old clicky Zippo.

"If you hear gunshots, that's probly just me. And y'all need to stay north of my house unless you know I'm not hunting. I don't want to accidentally shoot one of you. Deer season ain't 'til later in the year, but y'all may as well get used to being careful now. I hunt small game all year. I don't care what the government says, it's my property."

"OK." I've never been anywhere near a gun, let alone heard one in real life. The idea that one of us might actually get shot gave me chills. "Stay north of the house."

"Now, that old pole barn still has some of my junk in it, but I'll be getting the rest of it out here in the next week or so."

"We appreciate it. Thank you so much for letting us use it. We'll take good care of it."

"Not much you could do to it, it's pretty sturdy," Jack answered. "Roof don't leak, and the walls are solid. That reminds me, lemme show you where y'all should dig your outhouse." He started walking down the path toward the old pole barn.

Outhouse?

That's a bathroom, isn't it?

I'd forgotten we'd need one of those.

5

Well, That Went As Well As Could Be Expected

So yes, I did end up building our outhouse. It wasn't as difficult as I thought it would be, thanks to the Internet. Several vendors sell prefab outhouse kits on the internet. Mother earth bloggers explain the underlying concept and strategies in useful detail, so you can make a solid plan for how to handle the waste. For example, did you know you have to move the outhouse every so often, depending on how often it's used? It really can fill up. And ash from our campfire can be used to make it smell better. You just dump a cup of ash down the hole after your business is done, and it won't smell so bad. At least, that's what the Internet promises. Anyway, Jack was kind enough to lend me the digging tools. I almost asked my friends for help but then decided, why not hog all the fun for myself? Ha ha!

I also dug the post holes for the clothesline we'd need for our laundry, and asked Katie to bring the lumber we'd need to build them. It was so weird, remembering my grandmother hanging up the clothes in the summer time. When I was a kid, it seemed like a natural thing to do, but by the time I was grown up, nobody ever used clotheslines. Now we had come full circle. We really had no choice but to hang our clothes to dry, but it made perfect sense to do so. No machine needed, no electricity needed. Things like that make me wonder how cultural habits shift over time.

At long last, the surreal day we'd been dreaming of and working toward had become real. Liberation day! After weeks of semi-chaotic talk and action, I couldn't wait to see all the loose ends we'd been wrangling fall into place. And since every part of me was tired and sore from weeks of packing and moving and digging and building, I was also looking forward to being on vacation. I'd earned it!

Happily, the weather was perfect; cool, bright, and sunny. Twinkie arrived first, had already unpacked, and was setting the picnic table when I arrived. It was such a beautiful spring afternoon, I let out a whoop and hugged her.

"What a gorgeous day!"

"Yes! This is gonna be so awesome!"

With my arm over her shoulder, we turned to survey our new home-away-from-home, pointing out where we would grow flowers, plan a killer herb garden, and install the oversized outdoor hammock.

Stephanie arrived next, her tidy little compact car filled with tidy boxes and bags. She greeted us with her characteristic Mona Lisa smile and fist bumped each of us.

"So, Steph, we were thinking of tying up the hammock to those two trees there."

"If I were you, I wouldn't pick a spot downwind of the outhouse."

"Ah. Good call." That's why I like Stephanie. She doesn't mince words, but she'll never steer you wrong.

Stephanie walked over the outhouse and opened its door. I saw someone had already installed magazines, an air freshener, and pink silk flowers next to my LED lantern.

"Nice. Was this outhouse already here?"

"No, I built it from a kit."

"You built this yourself? Wow. Nice work." That was a huge compliment coming from Stephanie. I beamed.

Stephanie was unpacking her car when Maggie and Breanna pulled up. I knew this wasn't Maggie's first visit here, because there was already so much stuff in the pole barn. Even though she drove a big-butt SUV, it must have taken her six trips to carry everything over. The left wall of the pole barn was stacked high with bulk food cases, domestic supplies, and various instruments of travel comfort and luxury. At this point, I wished I had thought to organize the pole barn into rooms before we moved all our gear in.

Apparently, this was Breanna's first visit to the property. While Maggie and I started hauling the last of the supplies from Maggie's SUV, Breanna slowly walked toward the pole barn, looking all around.

"Wow, this is… primitive."

"What did you expect?" asked Stephanie.

"Uh, well you called it glamping. I thought it was an actual house. That looks like a barn."

"It is a barn."

"Where's the bathroom?" Breanna asked, concerned.

I pointed to the outhouse. "It's over there."

Breanna's expression turned to concern. "Where's the other bathroom?"

"Breanna, do you know what barns are?" Stephanie asked condescendingly.

(Technically, I almost decided to build a second outhouse, because five women are not traditionally known for sharing one bathroom very well (or at all), but since this outhouse was ONLY for voiding, and not for doing hair, fixing make-up, shaving, trying on clothes, or practicing selfie faces in the mirror, I figured the chances of a traffic jam would be pretty slim. I also figured, in case there was an actual potty emergency, squatting behind the outhouse wouldn't be a drastic change from actually sitting in the outhouse. To be honest, though, digging a second six-foot-deep hole was a seriously unappealing proposition after digging the first.)

Maggie interrupted Breanna's sinking horror with a plaintive call. "Breanna! Come help me with Snickers!" She was back at her SUV, holding a heavy-looking cat carrier in one hand, and trying to yank out the litter box with the other. "Come keep him company in the barn while I finish unpacking. Don't let him out."

I like cats. I kind of like Snickers, but he's been spoiled his whole life, so he'd become a prissy little furbeast. I really didn't mind that Maggie brought him; in fact, I was glad for the novelty of a second species in our social experiment, even he sleeps all day. He is cute and cuddly and makes funny noises when he plays. But Maggie said repeatedly we must never let Snickers go outside. She raised him as an indoor cat who would certainly get lost and die of exposure in the wilderness if he ever escaped the barn. And I don't want to see Maggie in a panic if her baby escapes. She's the closest one in our group to an actual mother.

Maggie, Stephanie and I finished bringing the last of Maggie's gear into the barn. I plugged in the white LED Christmas lights Katie and Twinkie had strung up to the rafters, then closed the big barn door. Suddenly, we were in some sort of magical country prom-dance warehouse, surrounded by sweet twinkle lights and stacks of cardboard boxes that reminded me of hay bales.

"It's so pretty!" Twinkie exclaimed.

"Looks like we could have us a hoe-down in here!" crowed Stephanie. "Now all we need is some moonshine and a fiddle."

Meanwhile, Maggie was cooing at her cat, curled up in back of the carrier. "Come out here sweetie, it's OK." A tubby orange blur darted out to the one gap in the cluster of boxes Maggie couldn't pull him out of.

"Maggie, want to open up his food? That'll bring him out," Katie suggested.

"Yeah, that's a good idea." She stood up and started poking through her many boxes. "Here." She pulled out a can of soft food. "Oh no... I didn't bring a can opener."

"Uh..." I racked my brain for where mine is, then realized it was stowed in Twinkie's garage with the rest of my kitchen gear. "Twinkie, did you bring a can opener?" I asked hopefully.

"Shit. Maybe?" She rooted around one of the open boxes. "I have a bottle opener, but no can opener. I'm sorry."

"Isn't half our food canned?" asked Stephanie.

"Heh, yeah," answered Maggie. "I'm really sorry I forgot, guys. We're definitely going to need one."

"I'll drive back to town to get one," said Stephanie. "Do we need anything else?"

"Nah," said Twinkie. "We should be good."

Stephanie gave her a skeptical sideways glance, then left the barn, jangling her key ring.

"Hey," said Katie, "while I still have the ladder here, how about I set up your hammock?"

We all walked outside to a couple of well-spaced trees upwind of the outhouse, as Stephanie wisely suggested. The ground was just sloped enough that only one side needed the ladder to even out the hammock.

"Here, Shelby, you tie that end, and I'll get this end with the ladder."

"Sure, babe," said Shelby, "I can do a lot of cool and kinky stuff with a rope now…"

"Um…" Maggie said extra casually, "I think I'll go try to set up a campfire for dinner and s'mores."

"I think I'll come with you," I answered.

Back at the pole barn, we surveyed the scene before us and selected a location to build a fire. Maggie cleverly suggested we set up some logs as seats around the fire, which we found stacked up near the pole barn. We set up enough to accommodate our group, then sat and looked at the plain space in the middle of the circle.

"I don't know what to do next," said Maggie. "Put some sticks in the middle? How would we keep the fire from creeping outward to us?"

"Here, let me Google it." She sat closer to me as I searched for instructions. "First, we need to buy a fire pit…. No, we don't. The pioneers didn't have home improvement warehouses. Um… OK. We can use large stones from the surrounding area."

We looked around. No stones anywhere.

"OK, then…." I browsed another link. "We need to dig up a circle of grass where the fire goes, so it won't catch on fire." We worked the soil in front of our seating until it looked safely non-flammable.

"Now, we need tinder, kindling, and fuel wood."

"I didn't bring any of those."

"Nah, we get those from around. Dry dead leaves are tinder and they burn first. Kindling is little sticks, and then big sticks are fuel wood." I read for another moment. "Ok, we make a teepee out of little sticks, fill it with dead leaves, then add the big sticks later."

We easily grabbed the fuel we needed nearby, then arranged them artfully in the middle of our fire bed.

"Okay!" I said, triumphantly. "Now we light the tinder."

"Okay!" said Maggie.

We looked at each other.

"Did you bring any matches?" I asked.

"No, I'm sorry, I didn't bring any," Maggie replied.

"But you brought all those candles."

"I don't usually light my candles, they're just for decoration. I'm sorry."

"It's okay, Maggie. Twinkie might have one."

Maggie walked over to Twinkie, who was breaking up chocolate bars at the picnic table to make s'mores. "Hey, do you have a lighter, or matches?"

Twinkie threw her head back, closed her eyes and sighed. "I didn't bring any, damn it."

I walked over to ask the hammock team. None of them had a way to light the fire either.

"That's OK," sighed Maggie. "I'll just text Stephanie and ask her to pick some up." I waited while she tapped out her message.

We left our sad little fireless fire pit to check out the handiwork of the hammock team, who had just completed their installation. There between the trees stretched a deluxe cream-colored net with wooden slats on either end, almost as big as a twin mattress.

"Nice work, ladies!" I said.

"Thanks!" said Katie. "Want to be the first one to try it?"

"Nah, that honor should be yours," I replied.

"I've never been in a hammock before," answered Katie. She approached it and tested it with her hand. It swayed easily, and gave a little under her weight. She thought for a moment, tried to put a foot on it, then stopped herself.

"How do you get on?" she asked, staring befuddled at the hammock.

"I think you just kind of sit on it like a bed, then scoot into the middle," Maggie answered.

Katie did so awkwardly, swinging and bouncing as she slowly wriggled her way to the middle of the hammock.

"Hey, this is pretty comfy!" she said. "This could be relaxing."

"Awesome! Here, I'm gonna join you!"

"No wait!" Katie cried, but it was too late. Shelby stepped over to the hammock, sat down hard on the side, then leaned backwards onto Katie's legs. She swung her legs up and over just as Katie shifted her body defensively to avoid Shelby. The hammock swayed and flipped over, dumping both Katie and Shelby with a THUD onto the forest floor underneath it.

We started laughing. Shelby cried out in disgust. She sat up, dead leaves and a twig poking out of her hair. Katie pulled herself up too, her face smudged with dirt.

Breanna comes out of the pole barn toward us. "Hey, will we be eating soon? I'm hungry."

"Soon," said Maggie. "We're just waiting for Stephanie to come back with matches so we can light the campfire."

"I can't wait that long, I'm so hungry," Breanna whined. "Is there something I can eat now?"

"Not without a can opener," I replied.

"Sure we do," answered Maggie. "We have so much food." We followed her to the mountain of boxes inside the pole barn.

"Here," she pulled a bag of dried mangoes out of an open box and handed them to her sister.

Breanna tried ripping the bag open, but tearing at the "easy-open" slit on the side only removed the top strip of the bag without opening it.

"Do any of you have scissors?"

We looked at each other hopefully for a moment, but the hope quickly faded. Shelby pulled her phone out and texted Stephanie.

"I bet she's gonna love another request," I smiled awkwardly.

Shelby's phone buzzed. She looked down at it. "Yeah. She asked us if we actually packed anything."

"Wait," Twinkie reached into one of her boxes and produced a kitchen knife. "See, we don't need scissors." She handed the knife to Breanna.

Breanna took the knife and tried sawing into the big bag of mangoes. The knife slipped and sliced her finger open.

"Yaaaaaa!" Breanna yelled in pain, waving her wounded hand violently, flinging blood everywhere. She dropped the still-closed bag of mangoes onto the floor. We cried out in disgust, spun and stumbled away from Breanna's splash zone.

"Stop shaking your hand!" yelled Katie. "Just calm down!" She reached over to Breanna's bloody hand and applied pressure to slow the blood flow. "Where is the first aid kit?"

Maggie, Twinkie and I looked at each other for a moment, each in turn shaking our heads in embarrassment. I started laughing, drunk with defeat.

Katie sighed. "Better ask Stephanie to bring us one. Breanna needs antiseptic and a bandage."

I pulled out my phone and texted Stephanie.

ME

Hey, we need a first aid kit ASAP plz

STEPHANIE

You're fucking kidding me

ME

Not kidding. Sorry

It was soon apparent from the length of time Stephanie was gone, that we'd made her backtrack to town at least once. She returned shortly before sunset, finding us huddled tiredly around the unlit campfire, bruised, bloody, and dirty.

"You guys are shitty packers," she said. "You owe me one."

"You're right," I conceded. "You can have all the s'mores tonight."

"I'll settle for a double bourbon and coke," she said, and handed me one of her bags with all the supplies we requested.

I handed the first aid kit to Maggie to patch up Breanna. "What's in the other bags?" I asked.

"A few necessities I wanted to make sure I had here, even if you guys didn't pack it," she answered. "Toilet paper, tampons, rum, Coke, and a knife to stab anyone who asks me to go back to town today."

We started a cozy little campfire as the sun disappeared behind the horizon. Twinkie brought out skewers, hot dogs, buns, condiments, graham crackers, and a bag of marshmallows for the s'mores. Breanna looks around to each of us, confused.

"Don't we have any salad?"

Stephanie threw her head back and laughed maniacally into the night sky.

6

Nesting

I'm glad to report a drastic decrease in ridiculous mishaps after that first day, which was good because they were a bit demoralizing. By the end of the first day, we still hadn't set up hot water, a shower, or bedding. So we fell asleep that night in our grubby clothes, our tired bodies curled up on folded blankets over the hard barn floor. Our world smelled like earth and hay and old wood.

So the next day, having learned this literally hard lesson in what conveniences we'd been taking for granted, we worked together to restore those blissful conveniences in our new home as soon as possible.

Katie, Maggie and I sifted through my book on camping techniques over our cold, simple breakfast of fruity granola bars and bottles of tea. We selected a shower area under a tree near the pole barn. Katie strung up a hula hoop with a shower curtain hanging off it, and a hook to the branch to hold the solar-powered shower bag I bought. I could see the ground underneath would get nasty muddy, so I added cement path stones to the list for town.

"Add a few pressure-treated two-by-fours to your list, Emily," called Katie. "refilling this shower bag will be a bitch unless you have some way to climb up to it. I'll make you a few steps."

"Katie, you're awesome. I don't know what we'd do without you," I replied. "Sure you don't want to live here?"

"Yeah, I'm sure. But I'll keep coming back to visit. This is a crazy cool project and I want it to work." She grinned at me.

I grinned back. "Thanks! We want it to work too, so we appreciate your help."

Behind me, the side door to the pole barn squeaked open. Shelby, finally awake, was trudging out stiffly. She yelled back into the barn, "OK, I won't!" then closed the door behind her. She looked tired and bedraggled.

"Katie, are you about ready to go home?" She said.

"What were you yelling into the barn?" I asked.

"That I won't let Maggie's cat out. Can we go home now? I want a shower..." She looked up at Katie's handiwork, the plastic bag of water hanging from a tree. "...In my bathroom. Please." She offered up her most plaintive puppy-dog expression.

Katie smiled, unoffended. "Sure. Just let me grab my stuff in the barn." We walked over to the barn and opened the door. As soon as we did, we heard "Don't let the cat out!" from Maggie.

Stephanie, back in her corner of the pole barn, was on a ladder, tying something to a rafter. "Mags, how about if I tie up your cat? I think that would help."

"No, he wouldn't like that. You will just have to be careful."

"Electric fence?"

"No!" Maggie yelled.

We said goodbye to Katie and Shelby, then I walked over to Stephanie's corner. She was tying up her own hammock to a rafter with a tarp and rope.

"That's a good idea," I observed.

"I'm not the best hammock hanger, but it will do," Stephanie replied. She tied the last rope and climbed in to test it. She swung gently back and forth for a moment, eyes closed, then sighed.

"I'm gonna sleep well tonight."

"Oh, a hammock instead of a bed? I want one!" called out Twinkie from the other side of the pole barn. "Will you make me one?"

"I'd like one too," I added.

"Sure, I can do that. Pretty sure we have enough canvas."

"I have an inflatable mattress around here somewhere," said Maggie. "I got one for Breanna, too."

"I'd rather have a regular bed," Breanna replied. "At least a full size."

Stephanie opened her eyes and looked at me. "Will somebody shoot her already?" she muttered.

I mouthed NO and shook my head, then went to see what Twinkie was doing.

Twinkie was busy arranging a kitchen out of the workshop area along the left wall. She'd covered the top of the plywood worktable with adhesive vinyl to make it smooth and clean, more like a kitchen countertop. The other wood surfaces were freshly scrubbed; the smell of Murphy's oil soap was heaven to my nose. Near the outlet, she placed a hotplate and a coffee pot.

"Look," she said. "We have plenty of space for a microwave too. I'll bring mine in the next time we're in town."

"Mmm, microwave."

She waved slowly around to the shelving above and below the workspace, some of which held handsome color-coordinated plastic trays. "We'll keep the utensils here, dishes and cups here. Kitchen tools here. This whole section is for food. We can't fit all of it on the shelves, obviously, but it'd be easier to use what's already opened."

"One box of pop-tarts at a time."

"Exactly."

"Are you putting in a sink, too?"

"Nah, we'll wash dishes outside at the water pump. Use one of our buckets for washing. I don't want to bring water in here if possible, it'll get muddy in here, and that's nasty."

"Good call." After noticing that our current shower setup could potentially leave its bather muddier than when she started, I was eager to keep as much of the ground dry inside the barn as possible. I realized it would be a weird adjustment, getting used to avoiding making and tracking mud everywhere. Out in the real world, there is no mud.

Or is that backwards?

"So, what can I do to help?" I asked.

Twinkie discreetly pointed toward Maggie, several feet away on the other side of me. She was poking through fort of randomly labeled second-hand boxes and quietly talking to herself, surrounded by a halo of assorted gadgets, boxes, and bags.

I looked at Twinkie and nodded in acknowledgment.

Maggie is a Stuff Person. And by that, I mean she's kind of a hoarder. She's not selfish at all. She'd give anybody anything, pretty much, except for her nicer jewelry. But stuff consumes her life. She's been that way as long as I've known her. It was how her parents showed affection to her, especially during and after their divorce. She and her parents were always getting some kind of new game or toy or clothing or tool, to where both her mom's house and dad's house were stuffed. A lot of it would sit on top of piles with their tags still on. Some rooms had been reduced to walkways between mountains of random things.

She's been grown up for a while, living on her own, but she's still a collector, a constant searcher for something to make her feel less lonely, more pretty, more complete. A sucker for 'As Seen on TV' gadgets, matching seasonal decorations, exotically scented skin care products, electric dispensers, and complicated cat toys. She is also a big fan of buying groceries in bulk, more than she could ever use, which is a big reason why we were able to move out here so comfortably and quickly. (Even if she didn't have an enormous stash of supplies, we'd have still invited her. She's our sister, Twinkie's and mine. We've always been together.)

I sidled over to her and smiled carefully. She seemed to be a bit overloaded, psychologically. Faced with 1,000 things to look at and re-organize, her goal was lost to a tidal wave of materialistic reverie. Twinkie and I witnessed this a few times a year, usually around Halloween and Christmas.

"Hey, Maggie, did you find your inflatable mattresses yet?" I prompted her casually.

"No, but I did find this, have you seen it?" she replied, holding up a shiny ceramic jar in trendy earth-tones. "It's a scented wax warmer. We just plug it in and pretty soon, the whole place will smell like an evergreen glade."

"Awesome," I answered gently, silently noting the irony of producing that odor out here in the forest. "Let's put it back in the box for now. I have an idea. Let's move the food boxes closer to the kitchen, and we'll move the non-food stuff over next to your corner. And then we'll look for your inflatable mattresses and set them up."

"Sure." She put the wax warmer back into the box, then pulled out a big puffy C-shaped thing.

"Here is an airplane pillow, I thought it might come in handy in the hammock outside."

"Okay." I opened a box that said *Pork & Beans*, found that it really was a case of pork and beans, then carried it to the newly designated food pile.

She held up blue plastic donut with a red ball inside. "This is Snickers' favorite toy. See, he can swipe at the ball with his paw, but he can't ever get it out, it just spins around the ring. He loves it."

The whole thing suddenly seemed a bit sad and pathetic. Neither the cat nor the ball has any freedom.

"Maggie," I interrupted. "Here, let's finish this box later. We just need to put your mattresses together first." I reached over to close the cardboard box, then one of the box flaps smacked my hand. I looked in to find Snickers in the box, ready to fight for his new territory. We laughed and decided to work around him.

It took us almost an hour to sort the boxes, but we finished, and found the inflatable mattresses she bought for herself and Breanna. I'd never seen anything like them before. They were fancy, very durable, topped in soft green velvet. And they were huge, like full-size beds. We unfurled them, momentarily assaulted by their sharp plastic odor. I peeked around until I found the valve. It was way too big for a mouth to go around them.

"How do you blow these up?" I asked, confused.

"You hook a battery powered pump up to it. I bought one, it's around here somewhere…." Maggie walked over to the sorted pile of non-food items to begin a fresh search.

I need a break from this, I thought, and wandered back towards Twinkie and Stephanie. They were still working in the kitchen area to organize the huge supply of food.

"How's it going? Got anything good?" I asked.

Twinkie pointed toward a case of canned chicken chunks.

Stephanie waved toward at a collection of dried cranberries, raisins, the remaining mangoes, cherries, blueberries, and apricots.

Twinkie waved her hand melodramatically toward the lower shelves, which were full of boxes of instant potatoes, pasta kits, noodles, soup mixes, and cereal. Just add water (or reconstituted dry milk).

Stephanie held up a box of wine and chuckled.

"We have ten of these."

"All right!" Twinkie cried joyfully. "Pop that bad boy open!"

Stephanie laughed again and pulled out the spout from the box. "What the hell, the apocalypse is nigh anyway," she said, then poured each of them a cup.

"Want some?" offered Twinkie.

"No thanks," I answered. "I'm gonna go read for a bit." I felt tired, spent, ready for some quiet time. My introvert's social cup overfloweth.

Stephanie yelled out, "Breanna! Hey! How about you get off your butt and unpack something. You've been laying there all day." This was true.

"I don't know what to do," she answered. But she slipped her phone into her pocket and wandered over to Maggie's non-food supply stash.

"But don't move those boxes around," Stephanie called to her. "I like my wall." The stash occupied the space between Maggie's and Stephanie's corners in the back. Stephanie had arranged some of the boxes closer to her side to form a shoulder-high wall.

I looked up from my book when I heard boxes shifting, to see if Breanna was deconstructing Stephanie's wall. Breanna was forming a makeshift station out of cardboard boxes next to the other outlet in the barn. At her feet were a computer monitor and a video game console. She rested the console and monitor upon the boxes against the wall, then pulled the Christmas lights out of the socket.

The barn went completely dark.

"Hey!"

"What the hell?!"

"I can't see, turn the lights back on!"

"I let them go, I can't find them!" yelled back Breanna.

"Hold on, I'm coming." I yelled. I vaguely knew where they'd be dangling.

"Aaah, I hate the dark!" Twinkie cried out. I heard her scramble-stumble to the side door and open it. Light flooded the front of the barn.

"DON'T LET MY CAT OUT!!" Maggie yelped.

With the added light, I was able to spot the dangling light cord and plug it back in. The barn again lit, Twinkie closed the side door. I looked at Breanna standing next to the outlet with the console plug in her hand.

"Well, that was retarded," said Stephanie.

"Stephanie, just shut it." Twinkie shot back.

"Here," I caught Breanna's attention. She looked stricken. "Look, see, you can plug the console into the plug of the Christmas lights, so we have enough space for both." I looked over to Maggie. "Did you bring a power strip?"

"I don't know," Maggie responded tiredly. "Probably not." She was crouched down, searching around the barn for her cat. Breanna finished plugging in the console and monitor and settled in to play.

I knew Stephanie was pissed off and well into her third cup of wine, but I wanted to do anything to improve the peace in the barn. So I asked her to help me set up the canvas partitions. We spent half the afternoon stringing the ropes to the poles, then stringing the tarps up. The canvas came with reinforced eyelets so we could peel them back like curtains if desired. The effect was that each of us had a private compartment made of blank canvas.

That accomplished, I escaped with a book and a lawn chair to a welcoming clearing in the forest nearby. I was so glad to finally feel solitude again, and basked in the idea of having a comfortable, private place to sleep too. I spent the rest of the afternoon lost in my book, which was incredibly refreshing. Thankfully, everyone else was quiet too.

That evening after a dinner of queso blanco nachos with shredded chicken that we'd grilled over the campfire, we discussed what to call the pole barn, because 1. we agreed that 'pole barn' sounded too unappealing, and 2. Stephanie said the next time she heard the word "glamp," she was going to stab one of us. (Of course, I'm pretty sure she wouldn't actually do that. She just has a hyperbolic way of making her point. But I have no interest in seeing how far we can push her buttons.)

"Well, how about 'homestead?'" I asked.

"No thanks," Stephanie answered. "Homestead was the name of my high school. How about 'Ground Zero?'"

Twinkie interjected. "No, we're being serious."

We went around and around like that for a while before settling on calling it the campsite and going to sleep in our new compartments. I laid in my hammock thinking about the day, and realized a few things.

One is, we really are different people with different priorities. I never thought of us that way before. I love language and reading, but Maggie and Breanna couldn't care less. I don't even understand how people could not love the written word. In all those boxes we went through, Maggie didn't have a single book.

The other thing I realized is that, in our discussion of what to call it, all the proposed names suggested a temporary situation. None of us really seemed to be emotionally or psychologically investing ourselves here. I knew we weren't planning to be there forever. And I knew we hadn't been there long enough to be settled. I just… wanted the others to feel comfortable doing this. I wanted this not to be a huge mistake.

Suddenly overwhelmed by a sense of unease, I climbed out of my hammock, slipped on my shoes, and snuck outside.

The cool night air immediately kissed my face. The sounds of crickets filled my ears. My eyes widened and relaxed to let in the moonlight.

I took a few steps out and breathed deeply, smelling freshly chopped wood and spring leaves. I began to feel grounded again, because I felt like, in that brief moment, I had let go of everything that was bothering me, and was free to feel nothing but what was all around me… peace.

This is why we're here, I thought happily.

Of course, it wasn't long before other reasons to live 'off the grid' started piling up.

7

Drama Check, 1, 2, 1, 2

After about a week, we'd managed to work out a shower/lights/meal/chore schedule smoothly enough. But, as we'd suspected, there were enough of us to divide the daily chores so nobody spent more than a couple of hours actively working. Imagine that, exchanging an eight-hour day plus chores for a three-hour day including chores.

Even our bedtime routines changed naturally to more closely match the rising and setting of the sun. We never had more than a cozy campfire or Christmas lights to chase away the darkness of night, so our natural Circadian rhythms knocked most of us out by 10:00 pm. We awoke each morning refreshed, just in time to watch the sun rise to birdsong.

The upshot was that we each had a lot more time on our hands, but weren't sure what to do with it. On one hand, Stephanie and I, the resident introverts, were reeling from the unrelenting human contact. We spent a few hours each day on the hammock outside, out in the woods, or in the hayloft, which turned out to be a cool place to relax.

On the other hand, Breanna, Twinkie, and Maggie were going through serious TV withdrawal. Their original plan had Twinkie recording their favorite shows, then the three of them periodically driving back to Twinkie's house to catch up. The problem with that was they actually had relatively few "favorite shows." Their normal routine was to leave the TV on, then watch whatever was playing (usually while they were also reading their phones or texting friends.) So with our new living arrangement, they'd run through a week's worth of recorded favorite TV on Mondays, aka "Show Day." The three would take Maggie's car to Twinkie's house, leaving Stephanie and I to veg out at the campsite in peace.

But that meant the other six days of the week, three TV addicts were jonesing for noise and drama, while the other two people preferred none. It started causing problems in odd little ways. Like, a couple of us would get into gossipy conversations about whatever, whoever – the topic really didn't matter—that would end up devolving into an argument, complete with raised voices, complaints, shade thrown.

One Show Day ended up particularly frustrating for everyone. A favorite character on one show was killed off in a season finale. The girls returned that evening in varying stages of grief: anger, depression, bargaining, even a bit of denial.

"Maybe he jumped out at the last minute!"

"Or maybe that was another guy driving his car!"

"I thought I read they renewed his contract for next year!"

Regardless of their current stage of grief, they were being loud about it. Meanwhile, to be honest, Steph and I didn't care.

"Guys, will you please take it outside?" Stephanie urged them, rubbing her temples like she had a headache.

"I'm not going out there, it's too dark," Twinkie replied.

"Then start a campfire," Steph said. "A memorial fire. Go spill some beer on the curb for your dead homie. Don't go away mad, just go away."

"Jeez, Stephanie," Maggie said quietly. "What's your problem?"

"You guys blast in here yelling about a dead imaginary friend, that's what," Stephanie retorted. "It's not even real. It didn't even happen. You're just getting upset over nothing."

"It's not nothing!" Maggie yelled. "Sorry we have emotions and care about people. Just because you don't understand, doesn't mean it's nothing." She turned in a huff and walked out of the pole barn. Twinkie and Maggie followed her out. Curious, I followed them to the door, to watch them climb back into Maggie's car and switch the interior lights on. I could see my friends, at least in the front seats, continuing an animated conversation, but about what, I was no longer certain.

Shortly thereafter, they all came back in, much quieter, but no less tense. I was in my room getting ready to read, but decided to make a cup of hot tea. Twinkie was sitting at the kitchen area, texting on her phone. When I approached, she looked up at me.

"Hey, I just got into a weird conversation."

"About your show? Sorry your dude died."

"Oh, thanks. No, one of my friends texted me and told me to be careful going out, that I might get arrested."

"What for?" I asked, perplexed.

"Being a Muslim," she answered.

"But you aren't a Muslim," I replied.

"My Dad was," she said.

"That shouldn't matter."

"I know. But Tom told me to be careful going out in public, and said I shouldn't go out by myself anymore."

I raised an eyebrow and shrugged. "Maybe that's a weird, offhanded way to ask you out."

"I doubt it," Twinkie replied. "I'm pretty sure he's gay."

"Yeah, but you're just so darn cute."

She smiled at that.

Just then, her phone vibrated. She excused herself; I turned to finish brewing my cup of tea.

"Hey, how's it going?" she answered. "Yeah, I'm fine, why?... No, I'm just out visiting family, the reception isn't good out here... What? Why?... What?" Her voice turned serious. I turned back to watch her.

"No I haven't… No not usually…. Yeah I know, my Jack says that too. It's just so boring…. Wow, okay…. My birth certificate? I don't know, I doubt it. How would I even get a copy of that?... No, I'm pretty sure I don't have one…. Okay. Okay…. Is that really necessary, just to go to the store?... That's crazy…. Okay, well, thanks for calling. I will. Bye." She ended her call.

"What was all that about?" I asked.

She looked at me woodenly. "Nothing," she said.

I looked back at her curiously, but instead of elaborating, she walked into her compartment and closed the curtain door.

The next morning, we all were back to our normal morning routine, despite not quite having the conflicts from the previous night fully smoothed over. Stephanie and Breanna were sleeping in; Maggie, Twinkie and I were preparing breakfast.

Twinkie was making pancakes at the hotplate when she heard her phone buzz. She answered it, then flagged Maggie to watch the pancakes while she left to take the call. I watched her walk outside, her face a picture of curiosity and concern. Several minutes later, Twinkie returned to the barn and plopped down into a folding chair near the kitchen. Maggie handed her a plate of pancakes and syrup. Twinkie didn't say thank you, which was unusual enough for Twinkie that Maggie did a double-take.

"Hey Twink, is everything okay?" she asked.

Twinkie sighed heavily as she chopped her pancake into bite-sized pieces with her fork.

"I keep getting calls from people who are sure I'm about to get deported," she said with tinges of concern and frustration.

"What?" Stephanie asked, lured into the kitchen from the final gurgles of the coffee pot.

"Three people since last night," Twinkie elaborated. "That was my old English professor calling me just now. He suggested I start wearing a gold cross when I go out."

"Oh, Twinkie!" Maggie cried. "Is it that bad out there now? We can't let anything happen to you!"

Stephanie was obviously still skeptical. "That doesn't make any sense. You're a natural born citizen. What could they possibly do to you? You can't get arrested for not looking Christian enough. That's crazy. You don't even wear a headscarf."

"Hey, I'm not making shit up, I'm telling you what my friends are saying," Twinkie replied defensively, then took a bite of her pancake. "And three of my friends just since last night called to tell me to watch my back and have a defense ready, just in case. They're seeing reports on the news."

"Yeah, which news?" Stephanie asked, still skeptical.

"I didn't ask, Stephanie," Twinkie answered. "Does it matter?"

"Is that a serious question?" Stephanie retorted, flabbergasted. "Does the source of the news matter? Is this the same "news" that reports our water supply is turning frogs gay?" she said, air-quoting for emphasis.

"This is serious business, Steph," Maggie exclaimed. "Stop making up stupid stuff."

Stephanie shook her head. "I'm not making that up. That's real. You guys are the ones being ridiculous. Making shit up just to get excited about it."

Maggie was turning pretty huffy by this point, but Twinkie remained calm. "Look. This is serious business," she said, nodding toward Maggie, which seemed to calm her down a bit. "But it's not like I *want* to be detained by the Feds, so I have no reason to blow this out of proportion. My friends said there was news about it, so that should be easy enough to confirm."

Stephanie's skeptical expression softened.

"So, do you want to help me confirm these stories?" Twinkie asked her.

Stephanie looked taken aback, then nodded. "Yeah, I would. We should find out if there's anything you need to be concerned about."

"Okay then. I'll fire up my laptop."

I was glad to see that all worked out. Once again, Twinkie deftly handled the personality conflict, managing to soothe both parties at the same time. And Stephanie, I knew from college, was a consummate researcher. I had faith she would get down to the bottom of the rumors.

Twinkie and Stephanie spent nearly an hour sharing the laptop screen, clicking and pointing and murmuring. By the end of it, Stephanie looked perplexed. I brought her a cup of coffee, which she gladly accepted.

"So?" I asked.

Twinkie shrugged, while Stephanie shook her head. "The more I read, the less it seemed like they were saying anything," she said. "If you read the news at face value, yes, there is an operation to remove "undocumented alien criminals," and nothing more. Sounds legit, right? Like, of course we'd want to do that. And there are glowing reports and analyses from the powers that be. Like, look at all the bad people we're kicking out. But social media tells a different story. It's full of personal testimonials of legal visa holders, even US citizens, detained at checkpoints or refused entry, and it takes lawyers to get citizens, *not even charged with a crime,* out of police custody. And who are the Feds focusing on? Anyone who *appears to be* Hispanic or Muslim."

"But it's not official," Twinkie shrugged.

"But it kind of is," Stephanie said. "They left the language ambiguous, on purpose, I'm sure. If Twinkie just looks the part, Homeland Security has the right to detain her for further investigation and/or 'processing,' whatever that means."

"I'm not afraid. Let them try to pick me up. I will sue them so hard…" Twinkie said with a wide-eyed, *don't fuck with me* look.

"Hey… I owe you an apology," Stephanie said contritely to her. "I accused you of blowing things out of proportion, but the fact is, you've been really cool about the whole thing. So I'm sorry."

Twinkie half-smiled at her. "That's okay. Thanks for helping me look this stuff up."

"So, the upshot is…." I asked hesitantly.

"We couldn't find any local anecdotes of detentions," Twinkie said. "Just isolated testimonials scattered everywhere, and very few details, because people are afraid to give their personal information on the Internet."

"'Everywhere' being a key word," Stephanie added. "Honestly, I think her friends are right. If Twinkie goes out anywhere, I think at least one of us should go with her, just in case."

"It's not fair," Twinkie blustered. "This is bullshit. This is against everything our country is supposed to stand for."

"I know," I said sadly.

"My family is nothing but good people," she added angrily. "They don't deserve us, if they're going to treat us like that."

When she said 'my family,' I assumed she meant Iranian-Americans, but I heard it as us, her friends.

If our own society is going to pit Americans against each other to the point where the powerful group jails or deports a whole minority group indiscriminately, we can't participate. We just can't.

But that means we're stuck here until it's over, right?

At that moment, it didn't seem doable. We were blowing through our food supply, running out of money, getting on each other's nerves, spinning our wheels.

8

Army Men

"Internet's still down."

They were the first words to cross Breanna's lips in two days. She'd finally gotten the message from three weeks of our collective passive-aggression that her constant complaining was not welcome. She also seemed terminally disinterested in helping us do anything. But, since she had nowhere else to live, and nobody would let her borrow their car to go to town, she settled into a ghost-like existence, either laying on her bed with her phone, or huddled near the console as if for warmth.

Stephanie ignored Breanna, despite the ripe opening for a snarky response. She had been more civil (in other words, unusually quiet) for over a week. I suspected Twinkie had a talk with her. Stephanie's commentary is usually witty, but had turned unacceptably cruel after a couple of weeks at the campsite. Twinkie has always been good at de-escalating fights and settling arguments. In her perspective, it didn't matter if Stephanie said what we were all thinking – sometimes it just shouldn't be said out loud.

"Did you pay your bill?" asked Maggie.

"Yeah, I remembered."

"Well, try again in a bit. Why don't you go outside for a walk? It's nice out."

Breanna sighed and trudged outside. She remembered, as we were conditioned by then, not to let the cat out.

We had settled into a tired kind of getting along. You know what they say about fish and visitors stinking after three days… in this case, we were all visitors, and we had all lived there more than three weeks by then. It was hard reconciling old comforting habits with the new environment and more people sharing the same space. There was no denying we were getting on each other's nerves, but nobody wanted to start a blowout fight either.

Twinkie had just returned from her morning shower. The rest of us were discussing the pain of using two outlets for five people, a kitchen, dressing area, and entertainment center, such as it was; lawn chairs in front of a computer monitor perched atop cardboard boxes.

"We don't have enough places to plug things in. The cords get all tangled up. I hate that."

"Yeah, can't we just buy more power strips?" Twinkie unwrapped her hair and rubbed it dry with her towel.

"We could plug in more stuff that way, but then we'd have the same amount of power stretched across more devices. You know how we run the microwave, the lights dim? That would get worse," I replied.

"Well, maybe if Little Miss Diva wasn't constantly playing video games and charging her phone, there'd be enough for everyone else," Stephanie said. She walked over to the wine box and dispensed the last of it into her cup. She deconstructed the box, splitting the cardboard (which we could use for kindling) from the plastic (which we couldn't).

"Come on, Steph, she's not using that much. And there's nothing else for her to do." Maggie fired back in defense. "I'm the only one who even talks to her."

"It's all beside the point," I said. "To get more power, we'd have to hire an electrician to come out here, and we don't really have the money for that."

"Shit," Stephanie uttered. She was bent over at our supply boxes, then straightened up. "We're out of wine." She grabbed her cup, downed it instantly, then made a beeline for her compartment.

"Why are we doing this again?" said Maggie tiredly.

My heart sank. I wanted us to escape all the fighting and tension and hard feelings by coming out here, but it followed us here. I remember thinking, maybe ultimately, we just aren't above it. Maybe we were all just being paranoid about the news and politics we'd been watching. Maybe Twinkie would be perfectly safe in town. Maybe we all suck, not just Internet trolls, but all of us. Maybe coming out here was a waste of time.

Instinctively, I reached for my phone, for the first time in days. My browser said no internet. I restarted my phone and tried again. Nothing. I hopped on my cell provider's app to make sure my account was OK, but that wasn't working either.

"That's odd," I murmured.

"What's odd?" Stephanie asked, coming back out of her compartment, her glass refilled. "And what's for lunch, Twinkie?"

Twinkie took a deep breath and glared straight ahead. She looked about to pop. "I don't care," she fumed. "Figure it out yourself for a change!"

Twinkie stormed out the side door. I followed her out the door and down the gravel path toward her aunt and uncle's house.

"Hey, you okay?" I called out.

"I'll be all right," she yelled without turning around. "Just leave me alone."

I re-entered the barn and shut the door as Maggie and Stephanie watched me. I shrugged in response to their quizzical looks.

"I think she just needs some space," I said.

"I think she's tired of feeling like a den mother," said Maggie.

"She's always the one to start the cooking. I thought it was because she wanted to," answered Stephanie.

"Not all the time," I explained. "She just feels responsible for everyone's comfort."

"Pfft," Stephanie replied. "The sooner she quits feeling responsible for everyone else, the sooner she'll be happy."

"What, and then she'll be like you, and not give a shit about anyone else?" asked Maggie, unusually brusquely.

"Well, yeah, pretty much," said Stephanie matter-of-factly. "What's wrong with that?"

Just then, Breanna returned from her walk.

"Hey, where'd Twinkie go? I'm hungry." She walked over to her phone, plugged into the wall. "Still no internet," she said sadly, and plunked down onto her lawn chair, hunched over her screen, seemingly willing her internet connection to reappear.

"I don't have any internet either," I agreed. "Hey Steph, you usually have the best coverage, will you check yours?" I asked.

Stephanie walked over to her compartment, then returned a moment later, twiddling her phone. "Nothing."

"That is strange," I said. "None of us have internet. I can't even log into my cell provider's app to check my account."

Even though we had all more or less sworn off our cell phones to avoid seeing the news we hated so much, being completely unable to access the internet felt unnerving, like we were lost or naked. I imagined Breanna probably felt lost *and* naked *and* bored to death.

Shortly after that, I was outside at the water pump washing our lunch dishes, when I heard a commotion – Twinkie running full speed toward me, yelling.

"Come quick! Get the others!" She panted. "You gotta see what's on the news…" she panted.

"What?!" I grabbed her shoulder with my wet hand.

"Just come look!" she cried out. "Come on! Hey, come out!"

Twinkie ran into the pole barn and called for the others to follow her, then ran straight back towards Jack's house.

Confused and alarmed, we chased her down the dirt path, up the porch steps, then into Janet's fragrant, vintage kitchen. The old screen door creaked and clapped shut behind us. On the kitchen table sat two half-consumed cups of coffee and a plate of homemade snickerdoodles. Twinkie called us into the living room.

Jack and Janet were sitting in their easy chairs, leaning attentively toward the TV screen. Twinkie waved us over to the couches so we could watch, but I chose to stand in the back corner.

The TV was overly loud and bright, dazzling my eyes after having avoided big screens for almost a month. A news announcer was describing raids of federal troops on several major cities in the US. You could hear the contained excitement in his voice. He kept mentioning "since the Homeland Defense Protocol was declared last week."

"What do they mean, Homeland Defense Protocol?"

"Ain't you been watching the news?" Jack said.

"No, we've been avoiding the news," Maggie answered.

"What's a Homeland Defense Protocol?" I demanded.

"Well, since those nuclear warheads were reported stolen –

"What?!" we all gasped.

"You really haven't been watching the news, have you. Well that's the sort of thing you miss. Yes, last week, the White House said some nuclear weapons were stolen by our enemy –

"Who, what enemy?" Stephanie asked critically.

"Well, they didn't say. Course everybody on TV's been speculating all week. Then a few days ago, the President decided that our biggest enemy was our own criminals, so he issued an executive order to lock 'em all up, all at once." answered Janet.

"What the hell does he mean by that?!" I asked.

"Criminals and undocumented immigrants, in the inner cities," she answered. "Drug dealers and rapists and so on."

"He said he's cracking down on the bad guys to protect our Second Amendment rights," Jack said.

At that, Stephanie rolled her eyes and gestured *seriously?*

"And protect our families and way of life," Janet added.

"Wait," I stuttered, "But it looks like they're just rounding people up and carting them off."

I pointed at the screen. It showed a continuous montage of troops in black full riot gear flowing out of armored vans and swarming through run-down urban residential neighborhoods.

Guns and flood lights pointed outward, making the scene look like a terrifying alien landing. The troops barked terse commands as they broke down doors, stormed dining rooms and dens, knocked unarmed men and women in their sweatpants down to the floor, cuffed them, kicked them, then dragged them into large vans.

"Yeah," said Jack. "Looks about the size of it."

"Have they found the stolen warheads?" Maggie asked.

"Nope."

"Do they seriously suspect that poor inner-city people are going around stealing nuclear bombs?" Stephanie asked dryly.

"Well of course it's horseshit," Jack retorted. "After a year of this craziness, I'm not even sure those warheads even existed. But when the government tells you we may get attacked at any moment, it's hard not be afraid of it."

Stunned into silence, we focused again on the broadcast.

"They're not even being charged with a crime," I pointed out.

"Nope," Jack said.

"They aren't even being read their rights."

"Well," Jack explained, "the President signed an executive order a few days ago that since we're living in a kind of a terrorist situation, because good American people are in danger on their own streets, they decided to round up everybody, then let people out if they're innocent. Saves time."

I leaned back onto the wall, completely flabbergasted. Stephanie was able to continue asking questions, thankfully, because I was speechless, my mind was so blown by what I'd just heard.

"So, they aren't being arrested?"

"Nope. Just taken into custody."

"What's the – (I could see her struggle not to drop the F bomb) – difference?" Steph sputtered.

"We don't know, honey," Janet replied. "We're just telling you what the guy on TV said."

"So, habeas corpus and Miranda rights just flew out the window?" I guessed from the look on Stephanie's face she was about to become speechless too.

"Yeah, something like that," Jack responded. "Because we're in a terror alert sort of situation."

That got her. Steph scrunched up her face and started shaking it in random directions, then facepalmed.

"I guess poor people no longer qualify as good Americans?" Twinkie commented darkly.

"Not the black ones," Jack replied. "Or Mexicans or Arabs either."

"Uncle Jack, how could you?!" Twinkie yelled, and started hyperventilating.

"Honey, we're not agreeing with it," Jack answered gently. Aunt Janet stood up and hugged her. Twinkie clung to her as her tears spilled onto Janet's shoulder.

"That's not the worst part of it," Twinkie said. She broke free from Janet to gesture toward the TV.

Jack changed the channel to the local station. A newscaster was announcing the successful "anti-crime" raid of our own hometown. This footage showed street after street devoid of people, except for a few police in riot gear patrolling the streets with their rifles out. The images on the screen looked like nothing we'd ever seen before in America, but the reporter made it sound like just another normal day. He said nobody was killed in the raid, and the police only had to pick up a few stragglers later in the morning.

"It happened last night," Janet said. "About three in the morning. They got almost everybody in one sweep."

"That's Katie's neighborhood…" I said, alarmed.

"We gotta go find her…." Twinkie cried, her throat tight.

I pulled out my phone and checked for service again, to call Nicole and Katie. "My phone is still dead."

"You can use our phone," said Janet. I followed her to the vintage plastic corded phone on her kitchen wall, then dialed Katie's phone number from my contact list.

"What does a fast beep beep beep mean?" I asked.

"Means the lines are busy, honey."

"We need to figure out what we're gonna do," I heard Steph say calmly.

"We have to bring them here," Maggie answered.

"Well...." Janet sighed. "I never thought I would see this in the US."

"Aunt Janet, why didn't you tell me they were gonna do this?" Twinkie asked. "I was here just a few days ago."

"Honey, I wasn't sure if it was actually going to happen, and it's not like they told us it would happen here. All the news sounds like a bunch of horseshit anymore anyway."

"I can't hear the TV. Can y'all take it outside?" Jack asked.

"Sorry, of course," answered Twinkie. We filed back out to the front porch.

"So...." Stephanie opened. "Communication is shut down, the police are carting off its own citizens by the truckload. Apparently we're now living in some fucked-up New World Order. Now I wish I hadn't put off getting my hair done last week."

"We need to start keeping track of what's going on," I said. "This is so messed up. I don't feel like any of us is safe anymore."

"You're white, you're safe." Twinkie retorted.

"Not as long as I'd die trying to protect you," I answered.

Twinkie suddenly hugged me. Then the rest of them closed in to hug us too.

"I'm gonna stay here and keep watching the news," Twinkie volunteered.

"Sure, Twink," I agreed. "They won't mind just one of us here, especially family."

Are you gonna go check on Katie?" she asked.

"Of course," answered Maggie.

We exchanged brief goodbyes with Twinkie and walked back to the campsite.

We decided that Stephanie and I would take Maggie's SUV into town to check on Katie and invite her to our campsite once again. It would have the most space to store any essentials she wanted to bring with her. I know the city well enough without GPS to drive to her apartment. Stephanie didn't say so, but I think she needed a break from the group.

Immediately upon entering the interstate toward town, we noticed bumper-to-bumper traffic in the other direction. Part of the southbound traffic jam included a long caravan of identical military trucks with canvas covers, the longest I'd ever seen. I turned on the radio, hoping for more information.

"Emily, I'm in no mood to listen to shitty pop music right now," Stephanie said darkly.

"Okay, but this station gives traffic reports on the hour," I replied, then tapped at the clock. It was three 'til.

I turned the music down low and sat in anxious silence, overwhelmed with worry for what caused the insane traffic jam, and for what we might see ahead. After the song and several jangly commercials, I turned the sound up to listen. Finally, the announcer reported a tractor-trailer jackknifed on the interstate a half-mile south of our campsite exit, blocking all lanes and forcing southbound traffic to a complete standstill. Emergency personnel had been dispatched to the crash site, but gave no estimate for when the road would be clear.

"We'll need to find a detour to get back," Stephanie said.

"Yeah. I don't know the back roads, do you?"

"No, and my sense of direction is terrible."

"Well, at least we know it's just a normal traffic jam," I said with some relief. "It's not like there's some crazy exodus from the city."

But a few minutes later, our car joined a mass of vehicles crawling toward the city limits, a river of brake lights blinking red. My heart leapt into my throat again. For thirty minutes, we crept and crept, looking behind us as the stream of cars behind us grew longer.

Finally, we reached what slowed us down – a line of police Humvees and cars, lights flashing, blocking all lanes. Police in riot gear lined up in front of it. An officer approached Stephanie's window and tapped it with his gloved finger. With his dark sunglasses and helmet, we couldn't see his face to read his expression. I turned off the radio as she lowered her window.

"This road is closed. Take this exit and turn around." He pointed toward the offramp just ahead.

"I don't understand, officer," Stephanie said with innocent confusion. "What's going on?"

"No one is allowed to enter the city until Homeland Security lowers the Threat Level," he answered sternly.

"Threat level? Did something happen here? My mom is sick, I need to check on her!" Stephanie cried out with grave concern. I wondered why she was lying, shocked she would lie at all, but kept silent.

"I'm sorry ma'am, no exceptions. Take this exit and go back where you came from. And wait for instructions from Homeland Security."

"But the interstate is blocked southbound, we can't go back the way we came," I said, and pointed further down the offramp, where cars were lining up for the clogged southbound onramp.

"Not my problem," the officer answered brusquely. "Move on, move on." He gestured very officially for us to take the offramp, and stepped back to end our interaction. Stephanie sighed, took the exit, then turned away from the intersection and the mass of cars waiting fruitlessly in traffic.

"Shit," Stephanie sighed. I'd never seen her look nervous before.

"Do you want to try to find another way in?" I asked.

"Hell no. I want to go back home. Fuck this shit."

"Okay."

"Um," she hesitated. "Do you know how to get back?"

"Of course," I said. "The property is southwest of us. So we go south for a while, then west, then we'll find it."

"You make it sound so easy," she replied. "I still get lost in my own subdivision."

"Wow. Seriously?"

"Yeah."

I sat quietly, casting my eyes around, noting the highway sign, the position of the sun, and landmarks to recall if necessary later. Then I remembered we were in Maggie's vehicle. I opened the glove compartment to find, crammed in with tons of other things, an old-school accordion map of the state.

"Check this out!" I crowed. "We'll find our way back with this, no problem."

"Holy shit," she said. "They still make maps?"

"Probably not, but Maggie has one, naturally," I answered. I looked at the map for a moment. "Okay, I see an easy way back to the campsite. Let's see. State Road 28 is just up ahead. Turn south on that."

"What do you mean south?! I don't know which way that is!" she barked, clearly agitated.

"Turn right. Jeez, chill out."

A moment later, we saw the road we needed.

"You're like, human GPS," she said with a nod of approval.

"The girls are gonna be pissed we didn't even try to drive into town," I said.

"Well then, they can try," Stephanie replied matter-of-factly. "But I'm not spending any more time wading through bullshit traffic and hoping we don't get lost in Bum-fuck Egypt."

"I guess you're right."

We drove for a few minutes in silence.

"Hey, Steph? Why did you lie to the cop back there?"

She glanced at me, then stared at the road ahead.

"I mean, I've known you for years, and you always say you pride yourself on your honesty. But that was just a plain old lie. And you sounded so convincing. Like you're an expert at it." I sounded a bit rattled. I bit my lip.

"That's true. I do take pride in being honest," Stephanie admitted. We drove for a moment in silence. "Look, here's my philosophy…. Never be ashamed of the truth. Truth is real. And I love telling the truth, because it's so rare anymore, it disarms people because they don't expect it. But… sometimes the truth can be twisted and used against you by assholes. And when I think assholes are gonna keep me from doing something important, I'm prepared to lie through my teeth, and not regret it."

"Hm."

A moment later, I recalled something, and smiled. Stephanie looked over at me.

"What are you smiling about?" she asked.

"I just realized something."

"What?" she asked.

"A few minutes ago, we were talking about the campsite... you called it home."

"Yeah, I guess I did. So what?"

I turned away to smile again to myself.

We came home to find Maggie rooting through the food boxes in a state of nervous energy. Breanna was curled up into a ball on her inflatable bed.

We entered silently, aware that the absence of Katie meant our mission was a failure. Maggie uprooted a bag of potato chips and peeled it open. She looked at us dully as she popped a couple of chips into her mouth. The cat, hearing the bag crinkling, jumped up onto the counter, hoping for a handout.

"Any word from Twinkie?"

She shook her head no.

We told Maggie about the road block and the traffic, and told her the accordion map in her glove compartment saved the day. She responded with a tired smile and a "that's nice," then carefully closed the chip bag and returned it to the pantry.

We all eventually wound up in our own beds and hammocks, silent. I think we were all worried, but didn't know what to say to each other. Who all did the police take? If they took Katie, where is she, and how the hell do we get her back?

I leaned over to look over at Maggie. She had curled up behind Breanna on her bed, spooning with her like they were little girls again. My mind went numb from the stress of the day, but I couldn't sleep, so I just laid in my hammock, staring blankly at my canvas partition. Katie and I hadn't gotten around to painting the pink lotus flower yet. The blankness of the canvas became painful to look at, so I turned my face away from it.

A while later, after sunset, Twinkie returned, bringing a blast of sound and life to an otherwise dead room. I arose from my hammock to greet her.

"Hey, ladies." She plunked a portable radio onto the kitchen/workshop counter.

That got Stephanie's attention. She walked over to the radio and turned it on.

"Since the internet is down, and there's no word on when we get it back, Jack gave us this. We can get the news from 99.9 FM, and these couple of AM stations." She reached over to click the AM switch. Crackly static overlaid a commercial for gold coins.

"Woo, gold coins! Followed by… hemorrhoid cream, home security systems, and CD players with clock radios in them! That's some hot stuff, right there!" Stephanie exclaimed sarcastically. She flipped it back to FM, dialed in to 99.9, heard a used car commercial, then shut it off.

Twinkie said, "We're still welcome to watch TV at their house, but they go to bed early. Besides, most of the cable stations aren't showing news or commentary right now. It's weird. It's all gone. I checked for hours. Some of the stations are just off the air, and others are just showing sitcom reruns and puff pieces on the President."

"Twinkie, did you learn anything new while we were gone?" I asked.

"Not really, except for the media blackout, which is creepy as fuck. Did you drive into town? What happened?"

As we relayed to her our experience on the road, we heard a car park outside our campsite. Maggie leapt out of her room, startling Snickers along the way, threw the door open, and ran outside. Hearing the familiar voices of my friends, I followed her out.

Katie and Nicole were stretching their arms and legs just outside Nicole's car, moaning and laughing with relief. Maggie closed in to hug Nicole, but she pushed her away.

"Not until after I pee!" She scurried off toward the outhouse.

"We were in the car all day," Katie said. "And she brought a thermos full of herbal tea with her. Which reminds me, I don't need to pee but I am so thirsty and hungry!" Maggie hugged her instead, then walked with her into the pole barn, offering the best of our food and beverages.

The pole barn door shut behind them, leaving me in darkness and quiet next to the car. I opened a door to find the backseat crammed with suitcases, bags and boxes. Nicole met me at the car and asked me for help carrying in their luggage. I looked at her for a moment.

"Looks like you guys changed your minds about staying," I said to her.

"Yeah," she answered with a sigh. "We tried to bring a lot of supplies with us. Hope you don't mind."

"No, you've always been welcome here. And thanks for bringing more loot."

Katie nodded. Her arms full of luggage, she walked inside. I grabbed my own load and followed her in.

As we fed our newcomers, we exchanged stories of our day. As it turned out, Katie and Nicole had been stuck in the traffic jam we passed on the way to town, and they weren't far from the front. It took a while for first responders to reach the scene.

"We saw your neighborhood had been raided on the news."

"Yeah, we saw it too, that's why we decided to leave town. Thank God I had just moved in with Nicole anyway, so I missed the whole thing."

"Why'd you move in with Nicole?" Twinkie asked.

"Remember when I said my water was tasting funny?"

"Yeah."

"Well, I didn't mind using a filter to drink it, but a couple of weeks ago it just turned brown and nasty, too gross to shower in, even. I told my landlord about it, and he said the water quality wasn't his issue to fix anyway, that the neighborhood was in bad shape, and city council refuses to fix the lines. And besides, someone had just offered to buy the whole building from him, so he was going to sell it and cut our leases out from under us."

"Yikes."

"So Nicole asked me to move in with her."

"What, and miss all this?" Stephanie joked, waving her hand at our canvas walls, cardboard boxes, and Christmas lights.

"I was tempted, I promise," Katie chuckled.

"I kind of needed her help anyway," Nicole explained. "I just got a letter from my school saying they were cancelling the student loan program. First I thought, if Katie can split the rent and utilities with me, I can afford to pay cash for one class per semester. But then I realized it would take me another ten years to finish my bachelor's degree. If I can stay here with you for a while, and host a few more yoga classes each week, I can save up enough in a year to pay cash for the rest of school."

"Yeah, that works out well," I said. "You're almost done anyway, right?"

"Yeah, 30 more credit hours."

Stephanie leaned over and whispered in my ear. "It's a shame people have to live in a fucking barn for a year to afford an education." I wondered why she whispered it, until I realized it sounded like a bad thing to live in a barn, but that's what were all doing.

Katie and Nicole also said they tried to call Shelby, but the phones were down by then. So they slipped a note under her door on their way out of town.

"All we can say for sure is, she was probably nowhere near the raids when they happened. No sugar daddies in the projects."

"Oh, Stephanie," Maggie chuckled.

By the time we'd finished catching up on the events of that long, surreal day, we were all limp with exhaustion. Breanna and Maggie shared Maggie's bed, to let Katie and Nicole use Breanna's compartment. I fell asleep quickly, so relieved that Katie was safe with us, under our roof.

9

Three Sisters

The next day, most of us were hungry for more information. Maggie offered to monitor the radio, as it was the closest thing she'd had to a TV for the last month. Nicole was able to fill us in on what she had seen, which wasn't exactly how the media was describing it – at least before they quit broadcasting opinions altogether.

"It's been, like, a complete whirlwind," Nicole explained as she stood up from the fire pit to stretch and swing her arms up to the sky. "So, the first week you guys were here, the government announced they were going to crack down on terrorists by refusing to let suspicious people enter the country. And by suspicious people, they meant brown people."

"So we heard," Stephanie said dryly.

"Then they said they were going to crack down on illegal immigrants and criminals. And suddenly we have army trucks IN TOWN. Driving around, sweeping neighborhoods. Then some of my friends started telling me some of their friends were detained even though they're US citizens, and weren't even being charged with anything. They call their families asking for help with an attorney, then that's the last we hear of them."

"That doesn't sound legal." I asked.

"That's what the Attorney General said right before the President fired him."

"Wow."

"Yeah," Nicole agreed, then assumed a sun salutation pose. "Then, the government announced a bunch of new import taxes. Mostly electronics and stuff, like they were saying cell phones and clothes and imported cars were gonna get a lot more expensive. The stock market went crazy. Everybody was either convinced the stock market was gonna make them rich, or crash. And the stock market didn't seem sure either, it went up and down and up and down."

"What do you mean, new import taxes?" Stephanie asked.

"I don't know, I don't understand the details. Then, just like they said on the news, they announce they're going to crack down on crime. But what I saw was, first they shut down social media, and I lost contact with my friends. Then they cleared out shitty neighborhoods. No offense, Katie."

"That's okay," Katie replied with a shrug. "I wasn't living there to impress anybody."

"How widespread is it?" I asked.

"What, social media being down, or the clearing out?"

"Both. Either."

Nicole shrugged her shoulders. "There wasn't any news at all about social media shutting down, so I thought the problem was just with my phone. As far as the clearing out, I heard that "anti-crime" raids were being conducted, but no numbers, no pictures until yesterday." She glided smoothly into a warrior pose.

"My guess is that there's "anti-crime" going on all over the country, that it isn't just us," Stephanie remarked.

"Makes sense to me," I replied. "Do you know anything about how many people they took away? Or what they did with them?"

"No, just that people were saying it was a clean sweep of Katie's neighborhood. A few city blocks' worth."

Stephanie kept shaking her head, lost in thought.

"This is bullshit," she finally said. "They're rounding up poor people like stray dogs."

"They can't keep them, not without charging them with a crime," Maggie answered.

"No, the news said yesterday that's exactly what they were doing, remember?" Twinkie said.

"Whatever they did, they did it in the middle of the night," Nicole said. "By the time reporters arrived, the raid was over, and all the reporters had to report on was the official statement from the DHS."

"But they can't be just hauling off American citizens and taking them AWAY, or whatever you're suggesting," Maggie said, starting to get huffy.

Stephanie stood up. "Maggie, the narrative you believe doesn't match the facts we're seeing. We know our government's been lying to us. So quit getting defensive and being ignorant."

"That's kinda rude, Stephanie. She's entitled to her belief. Why do you have to be right all the time? What is your deal?" Twinkie glared at Stephanie.

Silence filled the room. Stephanie stared at Twinkie, then Maggie, then looked away and sighed.

"I just want to deal with what's real," she said simply.

"Well, here's something that's real," Twinkie said. "We have no idea what's going to happen next, I'm afraid to even go back to town at this point, and we only have a few months' of food left."

"I can't handle this. I don't want to hear it anymore!" Maggie cried out, then fled the barn.

We sat for a moment in silence. I had a feeling Maggie's outburst had been boiling up inside her for a while. We knew well enough to give her some space for a few minutes.

"Look," I said, "I don't care if we really do have to start growing our own food, I don't want to take part in that craziness out there. Don't want to have anything to do with it. And Twinkie probably isn't safe at all anymore. So I'd rather just chill out here and wait for this all to blow over, than to go back now." We'd planned to plant a garden when we first arrived, but none of us had actually done anything about it. Oops.

"Well then, let's do it!" Nicole exclaimed brightly. "I brought a ton of seeds with me."

"Wow, right now?" Twinkie asked incredulously. "Isn't it too late in the year?"

"No it's not too late," Nicole answered. "Everything has its own season. It's always planting time for something." Nicole stood up, took Katie by the hand, then waved us to come out with her. Once outside, she immediately marked off a plot and directed us to get some tools and start turning soil.

Except, as usual, Breanna didn't come out with us. Nicole did a quick visual sweep, noticed, then asked about Breanna's whereabouts. Twinkie whispered something into Nicole's ear, then headed toward the pole barn. The rest of us started digging.

Then I watched out of the corner of my eye as Nicole tracked down Maggie, sitting in a clearing. She sat down next to her, put her arm around her. Nicole's energetic optimism and present-moment thinking was exactly what Maggie needed to cheer up. It wasn't long before Maggie joined us at our garden plot. Next, Nicole set Katie to the task of building a bunch of trellises, then sat at the picnic table with her seed inventory and books, working out which seeds to plant, when, and where.

Meanwhile, much to our surprise, Twinkie exited the pole barn with Breanna. They each grabbed a tool and started working the eastern edge of the plot together. It sounded like they were talking about TV shows, but I wasn't sure. We all glanced over at her a couple of times, but nobody wanted to jinx her unusual participation by pointing it out.

Maggie and I ended up working the western half of the plot, side by side, lifting sod up with pitch forks, then fluffing the rich, black soil underneath. Every few square inches, fat, pink earthworms wriggled up in surprise at being uncovered. I tried not to break any of them with my shovel. Nicole said they were a good sign that the soil was healthy for our garden. Maggie quickly overcame her initial squeamishness to see them as a positive sign.

"I know you guys don't agree with me," Maggie commented as we dug and tugged our way toward the center of the plot. "But if we don't listen to the radio, and we don't know what's going on out there, life is a lot more pleasant."

"I know what you mean," I admitted, "but we can't just stick our heads in the sand forever."

"I just wish it would all go away," she said sadly.

"I wish I had the guts to join a resistance movement or something, but I don't. I feel bad about not helping other people." I jabbed a clod of dirt in frustration.

"But you're helping us," she answered simply. "Look what you and Twinkie accomplished. We'd all be alone, hiding from the bad news in our own apartments and houses, getting fat off all the ice cream we're eating to make ourselves feel better."

"I thought you'd miss ice cream."

"I do. But I feel safer here, and I stay busier, so I don't need ice cream the way I used to."

"Speaking of ice cream," I said, "the worms remind me of that dessert you make with chocolate cookies and gummy worms."

"Dirt pie," Maggie chuckled.

"See, if you hid from the world, you wouldn't find crazy dessert recipes on the internet."

"No. But I would find more of what's right in front of me." She lifted her pitchfork to show me a clump of dirt with a triangle sticking out of it. I plucked it out and rubbed the dirt off with my fingers. It was an arrowhead, the first I had ever seen in person.

"Here," I said, handing it to her, smiling.

"You can keep it," she said with a smile, then turned back to her work.

That was a surprise.

We all continued to work the soil for the rest of the day, turning that big patch of grass into a bona fide garden plot. It wasn't until we stopped for the day that our muscles let us know how angry they were. We executed the evening's domestic chores together slowly and stiffly.

While we washed the dinner dishes at the water pump, Twinkie sighed.

"You know what?" she asked.

"What?"

"I feel better when we're busy doing something with our hands. It's when we're doing nothing, I feel uneasy and scared." She handed me a wet plate.

"Yeah, me too," I admitted. "And Maggie does too. She just needs to stay busy and focus on what's right in front of her. She's seemed really overwhelmed lately."

"I don't blame her," Twinkie replied, wiping her face with the inside of her elbow.

"And it probably isn't helping that her sister's pretty much shut down."

"Yeah, I've been feeling guilty about that," Twinkie admitted. "She probably feels really unwanted but there's no place for her to go. That's a shitty way to feel."

"She's not really doing anything to help herself. You can't blame yourself for that."

"I don't give myself all the blame. Steph's been giving her a hard time since the beginning."

"Steph gives everyone a hard time."

"Doesn't make it right." She handed me a cup to dry.

"She's really stressed, you know. She's not used to having people around all the time." Saying this, I realized the same could be said about me.

"Neither are you." (See, Twinkie knows me.)

"Well, that's true." I gazed outward to the forest. It always looks so peaceful. "But I always sneak off to read. Stephanie doesn't do that."

"No, instead she trolls people. You know what? To be honest, sometimes I don't understand why you like her."

I thought for a moment. "I like her because she has no shame."

"Isn't that a bad thing, having no shame?" Twinkie asked, handing me another dish.

"Not necessarily. Sometimes it's good. For example, when we were living together in our dorm room, I accidentally brought in fleas from my dad's apartment. I was so, so embarrassed, I hated to tell her, but I had to, of course. But instead of getting really upset about it, she just said "okay," and dealt with it. And that made my own shame about it fade away."

"Well, that's cool."

"And another time, we had an English class together, and some of the guys in our class started cracking really nasty AIDS jokes and talking about stereotypes. Stephanie stood up right there in class and told everybody she was HIV positive, and dared them to tell those jokes again to her face. It seriously shut them up. It even blew the teacher away."

"She has HIV?" Maggie asked, incredulous. She'd walked up behind us mid-conversation, unnoticed until now.

"I don't know," I replied, "and to be honest, I never felt like asking."

Maggie's look of concern held strong. "Well, we're living with her! We should know things like that."

"Uh," I said, trying to talk her out of making a big deal about it, but she'd already made several yards' progress toward Stephanie relaxing in the outside hammock.

"Stephanie, do you have HIV?" Maggie asked, point-blank, standing at the base of the hammock.

Stephanie looked blandly up from her book to gaze at Maggie. "Yes, Maggie, I do. And I need to tell you something else. I've been having sex with your cat."

"Stephanie!" Maggie exclaimed. "Ugh!"

"But don't worry, we're using protection, so he should be fine," Stephanie added, then went back to her book.

Maggie sputtered for a minute, then realized she'd been played and tromped into the pole barn. Twinkie and I chuckled.

"It's tough, you know," I say to Twinkie in Stephanie's defense. "None of us have been in this situation before. We're all trying to figure out our own ways to cope. Steph and I aren't used to having people around all the time. She tends to rely on snarky humor to vent. Breanna's not used to being constantly entertained by her boyfriend, or friends, or her phone. Maggie's not used to dealing with uncertainty."

"Or a lack of air conditioning," Twinkie added.

"Exactly. See, it's a wonder we haven't killed each other for the last ice cream sandwich."

"I thought we were out of ice cream sandwiches."

"See? I'm just saying."

Twinkie nodded, then looked at me and cocked her head. "So... how do we make this better for everybody?"

"Well, I won't mind being the only one listening to the news from now on," I offered. "We don't all need to listen to it. I'll pass on the important bits."

"Makes sense to me," she said. "It's either depressing or infuriating anyway. You can have it."

"Will you keep prying Breanna out of her shell? Make her be more of a part of the team?"

"Yeah, I think that's a good idea. I wish I had done that earlier."

"Don't worry about that. It wasn't as important then as it is now."

When we were done with the dishes, I hugged Twinkie, then took my dog-eared copy of *The Good Earth* out to the hammock to read until dusk. Seemed fitting for the day. We all went to bed early, and for sure, none of us had trouble sleeping that night.

The next day, Nicole divided the plots into sections, conditioned some of the soil to accommodate certain crops, then added Katie's trellises. She then directed us to plant the seeds. Some of them she had us plant closely together. It looked like they'd all be a jumbled mess, but Nicole assured us it would work out for the best.

"This is called Three Sisters," she explained. The beans climb up the corn and fertilize the soil for the corn and squash. Then the squash provides ground cover to protect them from weeds and keep the ground moist."

That's the kind of teamwork we should try to do for each other. How else can we apply that strategy, I wondered?

After Katie made cute labels for each section and applied them to the plot, we stood together to admire our handiwork. I felt excited, protective of it, and slightly overwhelmed by the responsibility.

My next task was to use our reference book for small-space gardening to estimate what our output would be (barring any disasters). I did the math, checked, then rechecked. It almost seemed too good to be true. But I couldn't find any holes in the logic, so I shared my estimates with Twinkie.

"Wow, that's a lot of food," she said, clearly impressed.

"Well, that's assuming the plants do well. Nicole seems to know what she's doing."

"Oh yeah," Katie said. "Haven't you ever been to her house? She goes all out, making mushrooms in her basement, compost in the back yard, homemade yogurt, all her own herbs and veggies. All organic. She's serious about this stuff."

"Wow."

"She even petitioned the city to lift the ban on keeping chickens within city limits."

"Wow. She fought the law?" I asked, impressed at Nicole's uncharacteristic immersion into city politics.

"Yes. The chicken law."

"Did she win?" I asked.

"Yeah, but after that, she went to a chicken farm to buy some and was totally grossed out by the chickens. She said they're nasty, vicious things. They poke each other's eyes out and stuff."

"Ew!" I exclaimed. Twinkie laughed at my reaction.

"But gardening, she's got in check," Katie said assuredly.

"The thing is," I added, "Is that we need to find a way to preserve all this food. We can't just eat a bushel of carrots for a week."

"I thought we bought canning supplies," Nicole answered. She had just walked over from the garden plot.

"Yeah, but I've never actually done it," I said.

"I made lime pickles once, but that's all," Nicole said. "They were awesome."

"We're not going to pickle everything we grow, are we?" Katie asked defensively. "Because if we do, I might starve."

"I'm getting the impression you're not a fan of pickles… but I might just be reading into it," I teased her.

"No seriously," Katie said. "Can we preserve the veggies without pickling them?"

"Of course," I said. Katie sighed deeply in relief.

"Aunt Janet cans all her vegetables," Twinkie said. "I bet she'll show us how, and let us use her kitchen."

"Have you ever tried them?" I asked.

"Yes, they're delicious. Beets, baby sweet pickles, —chill out, Katie-- corn, carrots, beans, green beans, peaches, tomatoes for chili… It tastes way better than canned food at a store. And some things you don't have to can, like potatoes and squash. Aunt Janet just keeps them in the garage all winter. She'd serve these at every family Sunday dinner."

"You're making me hungry," Maggie said. She left us for a snack in the pole barn.

"Nicole, how long before the first harvest?"

"About eight weeks, give or take a few days," Nicole replied.

"Twinkie, do we have enough to last us that long?"

"Oh, yeah. We have enough for three more months right now."

"Excellent," I said.

"But there is a hitch to that," Twinkie added. We all looked over to her, expectantly. "If we want the food to last three months, we're gonna need to start rationing."

"And there's another hitch too," Nicole admitted. "Some of the plants will be ready for harvesting in two months, but not all of them. Our food production will be low for at least twelve weeks, and it won't be at 100% until our compost heap is ready next spring. And honestly, some of the stuff we planted today shouldn't be harvested until next year. We should let them mature enough to harvest it regularly without killing it."

"OK," I said, "so we either need to ration or build up our food supply."

"We should definitely do both, if possible," Twinkie replied.

"Can we just buy more food? There's no reason why some of us can't drive into town," Katie said carefully. She brought up a point we've been trying to forget about.

"The problem with that is we don't have much cash left," I said. "We're saving it for bigger emergencies."

"A bigger emergency than running out of food?" Katie said. "What could be a bigger emergency than that?"

"What I mean is, if we can grow or find our food, let's not spend our money on it, because we can't grow our own cook stove or blankets or medicine."

"Uh, yeah you can," Nicole interjected.

"You know what I mean," I said. "We can do those, but not overnight."

"We could try keeping our own chickens..." Twinkie suggested, suspiciously tongue-in-cheek.

"NOOOOOOO!," Nicole cried. We all laughed at her exaggerated horror at the idea.

"Okay," Katie agreed. "What about hunting?"

Nicole wrinkled her nose. "I'm not sure I want to keep eating meat enough to hunt for it. I'm practically a vegetarian anyway."

"That's fine," Twinkie said, "But I freaking love meat."

I remembered my first meeting with Jack in the spring. "Jack hunts on his property. Maybe he'd hunt for us."

"Yeah, maybe!" Twinkie exclaimed. "He usually bags a couple of deer each fall, and his family eats that all winter. Sometimes he gives me deer steaks or deer chili. I'll go ask him." She patted me on the back, stood up, and walked toward Jack's house.

I looked back at Katie, Nicole and Stephanie. Stephanie frowned for a moment, then spoke up calmly.

"Okay... even though we're growing food and we might add game to the menu, I think we should do some rationing too. We don't want to end up hungry because our assumptions were wrong."

"I agree," I replied. "So far, we haven't limited ourselves at all. In fact, sometimes I think we eat just to be doing something."

"Some of us more than others," Stephanie added, nodding toward the pole barn, where Maggie was probably still there, stress eating.

Once again, I wished Stephanie would lay off Maggie, but she had a point. "Yeah. It's mostly Maggie's food, but she brought it to share, and we need to make it last."

They all nodded quietly.

"So, you guys agree on the rationing?" They nodded again. Rationing sounds like something you'd do in a crisis situation, which is something none of us want to acknowledge, let alone be in.

"So if she's stress eating, and we need her to stop, what should we do?" Katie asked.

"I know what to do," Nicole answered easily. "Yoga. It'll ease her stress without food. You guys could do it with us. It'll be awesome!"

"Uh…" Stephanie and I audibly waffled, but Katie agreed to join her.

"Good luck with that, Nicole," Stephanie said, then started toward the pole barn.

"Hey, Steph," I called out. "Let me talk to her about it, okay?"

"Sure," Stephanie answered.

"Shouldn't we put the rationing to a vote?" Katie asked, concerned.

"I guess so, but most of us just agreed to it anyway, and besides, we don't have much choice in the matter," I replied. "It would be a nice gesture though."

"We can do it tonight then, after dinner."

"Not before dinner?" I asked.

"Nope…. Better to talk about rationing on a full stomach, not an empty one," Katie replied wisely.

10

And We Thought Meals Were Hard to Pick Before...

Katie and Nicole prepared a yummy chili in the Dutch oven, with extra green chilies and a few jalapenos, and simmered it for hours over a smoldering fire we took turns stoking. Twinkie returned from her visit with her aunt and uncle, vibrating with her usual party-planner energy. She told us they were willing to do several favors for us, to help us out with our food situation, in exchange for occasional odd jobs we could do for them. We gathered together around the campfire while Twinkie unloaded the news she was so excited about.

First, Aunt Janet agreed to teach us how to can our vegetables the way we'd learn best – by direct experience. She proposed that two of us spend a day with her next week to get canning lessons with her green beans and tomatoes. In exchange, we'll be the ones doing all the picking, washing, and snapping for her, in preparation for the canning. Twinkie, Katie and I immediately agreed to do this.

Second, Jack was initially skeptical, but agreed to teach a couple of us how to hunt for ourselves, and offered hunting access on his property on the condition we would only take animals that weren't off-limits. He has a couple of extra rifles we can use. (I bet he had a lot more than that, but I wasn't curious enough to ask.)

This second offer was met with silence in our group. We fidgeted for a moment, glancing around, looking at anything but each other.

"We don't have to, you know," Twinkie said. "It's just an idea."

"How much meat are we talking about?" Stephanie asked.

"He said we could get about 50 pounds from one deer. He only kills one per season for him and his wife."

"Wow," I said. "Where did I get the impression that hunters kill, like, one every time they go out?"

Twinkie shrugged. "He only hunts deer for meat, not sport. He suggested we only kill one or two, but only if we have freezer space. And we might have plenty of space by then, especially if we prioritize eating our current frozen food."

"It's not so much how many animals we'd be killing," Nicole said. "It's that we're being asked to kill animals at all. To me, one is too many. I can't do it. I'd rather be a vegetarian." She looked each of us in the eye resolutely.

"Me neither," Maggie added quietly. "I couldn't go out and kill an animal, then come home to my cat like I wasn't a murderer."

I stayed quiet because I was hoping someone else would volunteer.

"I wish I could guys, but I can't handle it," Twinkie said. "I don't mind the way it tastes, but my dad showed me a deer carcass when I was a kid, and I was so grossed out, I threw up."

I looked at Katie. She just shook her head and looked away.

Stephanie took a deep breath and sighed. "Well. I guess it's on me then." She took the last swig out of her cup.

"Steph, you don't have to agree to anything you don't want to do," Twinkie said in a reassuring voice. "We're not asking you to."

"Be that as it may," Steph replied matter-of-factly, "we need more food, and green beans aren't gonna be enough. And nobody else is willing. I don't see that I have a choice, besides leaving. One less mouth to feed. That's our third option." She ticked off her points on her fingers, then raised her hands and shrugged.

"Don't leave," I said abruptly.

She looked at me.

"I'll do it with you." I stared back at her. Suddenly, silence except for the crackle of the campfire.

"We don't need two of us with murder on our hands," she said, somewhat sarcastically. She leaned over to the chili and stirred it.

"I don't have a problem with guns, or hunting, or gross things," I lied. "And I think we should always have more than one person at camp who knows how to do something."

This much was true. Volunteering to gather how-to books and manuals came naturally to me. To be honest, some of those reference books we'd been using at the campsite I had purchased years earlier, long before this scheme had been hatched. But I had been thinking lately, what if we need to look something up, but we can't do it? At that point, our internet access was still gone. So I had quietly promised myself to learn everything we needed to know to thrive out there, then record it if we didn't already have it written down. That's why I volunteered to learn how to do canning with Aunt Janet. That way, if somebody left, the campsite wouldn't collapse from a lack of knowledge or skills.

But that's not why I wanted Steph to stay. She's a butthead sometimes, but I feel better having her around. She's the kind of person who would slay a dragon for her friends. Dragons, deer…. When you're afraid of large animals, they're all the same.

"So, what's the catch?" Stephanie turned to Twinkie. "What do your aunt and uncle want in return for teaching us to hunt and lending us a couple of rifles?"

Twinkie started passing out bowls for us. "He said his deer population needed some pruning anyway. I don't know how he could know something like that, but he said if we bagged a couple of deer this fall we'd be doing him a favor."

Stephanie shrugged, accepted her bowl, and scooped out some chili.

"There is a third option Jack mentioned," Twinkie said as she took the ladle from Stephanie and filled her own bowl. "You're not gonna want to hear it."

"What?"

"Keeping chickens."

I started laughing. The rest of the gang looked at me like I was crazy.

"You guys," Nicole broke in, "you do NOT want to be raising chickens."

"That's why I'm laughing," I said, wiping my eyes. "You've seen the dark side of chickens." Just hearing those words out loud made me laugh again.

"Yes!" she exclaimed. "And now I'm trying to protect you from the horror that I witnessed."

"Surely it can't be that bad," Maggie replied. She served herself some chili and handed Nicole the ladle.

"Yes it is. They're vile little beasts, they have no compassion for their fellow chickens." This made me laugh even harder. Stephanie started chuckling too.

"Maybe they just weren't treated right. Maybe they need more love or something," Maggie surmised. But this time, I was out of breath laughing, and Stephanie was curled up over her bowl in laughter.

"Maybe they just need more love!" Stephanie squealed out between giggles.

"No, seriously!" Maggie exclaimed.

"Well, they need something to keep them from gouging each other's eyes out!" Nicole cried out. "That was so gross!" She jabbed the ladle ineffectually into the Dutch oven for emphasis.

"I don't know what you're talking about, Nicole," Twinkie answered, clearly in a state of neutrality between pro-chicken and anti-chicken. "Aunt Janet and Uncle Jack's chickens aren't eyeball-gouging savages."

That tidbit of information quieted us all, and gave me a chance to catch my breath.

"Oh yeah?" Katie said.

"Yeah. They have fresh eggs almost every day, and then once in a while, roast chicken for dinner."

Several of us murmured about the deliciousness of eggs, a food none of us had tasted in a month.

"Well, I love the idea of having a continuous supply of protein without having to kill something for it," I said.

Nicole nodded. "Yeah, if you guys can figure out a way to keep the chickens humanely, I'm good with it." She finished serving herself, then sat down.

Twinkie pointed her spoon at Nicole. "Okay, you're on then. Let's find out how they do it. I think that'll be a decent investment to make."

"Me too," agree Maggie. "I'll help with them too, if we have chickens. I love birds."

"Incompatible with loving cats, I imagine," commented Stephanie.

"This is true. But Snickers is staying in the barn," Twinkie reminded her.

"I'll help too," Breanna spoke up. We all looked at her. "I used to raise finches."

"That's true," Maggie chimed in. "Her finches laid so many eggs, she'd give the babies to the pet shop when they could fly."

"Wow," I blurted out. That sounded like a rousing success, way beyond what I'd ever tried to nurture, and that was spider plants.

I glanced over at Stephanie, ready to shoot daggers from my eyes to stop her from making a smartass remark. But she was just sitting quietly, eating her chili, and watching the scene unfold.

Maggie cleared her throat. "Sis, we'll be eating the eggs. Are you sure you'll be okay with that?"

"Sure," Breanna replied calmly. "Eggs are eggs."

"And the birds…?" Maggie continued gently.

"I love chicken," Breanna replied steadily, "with ranch dressing on the side."

"Well, that's settled," Stephanie said, looking at Breanna with a small, sincere smile. "Thanks for helping."

With all the hope we had for increasing our food supply in the near future, we easily agreed to ration our remaining supply of food on an honor system. Twinkie offered to do an inventory and figure out how to stretch out the food longer. Maggie didn't object, but the conversation seemed to deflate her somewhat. She went to bed early.

Later that night, I was laying in my hammock reading, when I heard rain tap on the roof, creating a lovely white noise that enveloped us. I put my book down and just listened for a few minutes. Then I slipped on my sandals, walked over to the side door, and cracked it open to look outside. Even though it was dark, you could see our precious garden in the distance, soaking up the water. The rain fell gently, no wind to disturb it.

A small part of me worried that our garden was doomed because I was helping with it. Even those spider plant babies Katie gave me died, despite her promise they were unkillable. Still, that small voice of worry was silenced by the peaceful scene before me.

Nicole walked up behind me and rested her head on my shoulder to look over it. I rested my head on hers, and she put her arm around me. And we just watched the shower surround us, blessing our freshly planted seeds with a chance at life.

"This is a good sign," she said quietly.

"Yeah."

She lifted her head and smiled at me, kissed my cheek, then said good night and returned to her compartment.

11

Watch Out for Snakes

A week later, early one morning, we heard a knock on our door. Twinkie padded over to the door to answer it, which in a way was an historic occasion – our first visitor. It was Aunt Janet.

"What are you girls doing, sleeping in so late! I been up for two hours already. It's bean picking time! So if you're gonna do it, you gotta get up now."

I overheard this and stifled a groan. I might not agree with her impatient schedule, but today, she's the boss. I rolled out of my hammock, rubbing my eyes, and downed the last bit of water from last night's glass.

Shuffling over to the water pump for a quick sponge-bath, I met Twinkie and Katie, similarly bleary-eyed. It was 7:00 am, not terribly early, but we had become accustomed to the relaxed schedule of the unemployed. None of us could say she was a morning person, that much was certain.

We washed, stretched, and grabbed a quick breakfast of oatmeal and coffee. None of us felt the need to change out of our sleeping clothes, shorts and t-shirts, since they're also the ideal clothes for working in sunshine and dirt all morning. Sufficiently caffeinated, we walked to Janet and Jack's house, listening to the songbirds praise the day.

Aunt Janet looked as bright-eyed and perfectly coiffed at 7:30 am as she would any other time of day. Honestly, she seemed perpetually motivated, her fuel I could never determine. We looked like bums compared to her. She met us at her front screen door, then led us out to her back yard garden with a collection of dingy old plastic ice cream buckets splaying out from her fists. She handed to each of us two of the buckets.

I paused to notice Janet's garden. It was huge for a backyard garden, with a footprint as large as her house. I saw six different plants as she explained them: squash, peas, green beans, potatoes, tomatoes, and cucumber. Each type was planted in a couple of tidy, straight rows along a flat plane, just like they are illustrated in the Peter Rabbit stories I read as a kid. I realized Janet's garden looked so much more formal than ours, and worried a bit if we were doing it the wrong way.

"Pick the beans, but mind you don't break the stalks," she instructed. "And leave the little ones and flowers alone. We have another round of pickin' left this summer. I'll come back in a bit to empty out your buckets."

Twinkie knew what to do. She crouched down at the fluffy beanstalks and buried her arms into the leaves halfway to the shoulders. It looked like she was milking it, except she kept dropping green beans into the bucket at her feet.

I crouched down a few feet away from her, down the line, then inspected the beanstalk. I could easily see what Janet was referring to; the little white flowers, the big broad leaves, and in the middle, clusters of fat, fuzzy bean pods. They snapped off the vine easily. In a moment, I was able to find my groove and ensure a steady stream of beans landed in my bucket. But it wasn't long before my ankles and knees ached from the crouching position. I sat down cross-legged into the dirt to continue my picking, infinitely more comfortable.

It was amazing how many beans were nestled in the vines. I would think I had sufficiently cleared a patch, only to look back and spy another handful of beans I had missed in the tangle of green leaves and stalks. It took several minutes to harvest the mature beans from each foot of garden row. But I kept picking, moving slowly down the line, filling up bucket after bucket. Janet followed behind us to replace our full buckets with empty ones, then carrying the beans back into the house.

About thirty minutes into the job, I heard laughter behind me. I turned to see Aunt Janet pointing and laughing in my direction.

"What's funny?" I asked.

"I never saw anyone pick beans just sittin' on the ground like that before!"

"Why not sit?" I asked. "It's really comfortable."

"Mostly because of the garden snakes," she answered with a chuckle. She replaced my nearly full bucket with an empty one then walked away, still laughing to herself.

I looked around for a bit for evidence of garden snakes, holes or movement or actual snakes, and felt skeptical; not sure if she was saying that to prank me, or if that was common knowledge to everybody but city folk like myself. I decided that I wasn't scared enough of garden snakes to return to crouching, whether or not Janet was telling the truth. But I couldn't help but notice Maggie stood up as soon as Janet said that.

It felt like we were out there for hours, picking and picking. At one point, Janet pulled Maggie away and directed her to pick tomatoes instead. The sun wasn't quite overhead when we finally reached the end of both rows. I lost count of how many ice cream buckets I'd filled, but felt pretty satisfied—and tired of picking beans. We stood up, stretched our legs, then walked back to Aunt's house with our final buckets.

Janet called us to the kitchen, told us to wash our hands, then offered us ham sandwiches and potato salad for lunch at a big wooden table with cushioned country chairs. While she finished lunch preparations, I looked over her busy kitchen. It was like a tiny museum of fads from three decades, none of them current. Beige speckled ceramic mushrooms stored flour and sugar on the counter. Hand-painted wooden signs implored us to Bless This

Mess and Kiss the Cook. Dusty Rose and Cornflower bonneted geese graced the walls above the counter. When she instructed us to pour our own drinks, I opened a cabinet to find a huge array of glasses etched with flowers, and tourist coffee mugs from half the states in the Union.

When Jack joined us at the table, she told him about finding us sitting in the garden bed to pick the green beans. The way she talked, that was the biggest news of the day, and scandalous news at that.

"Sitting! Whoever heard of sitting in the garden! Hoo-wee!" That was the first time I ever saw Jack smile and laugh. "Nobody sits to pick beans."

"It's more comfortable that way," I said in my defense.

"It may be, but the snakes!" and Jack chuckled again.

"I'm not afraid of snakes," I said. In truth, I was just skeptical.

"Heh heh heh. Just you wait." Jack winked at me, and reached for the potato salad.

To this day, I wonder which one of us was the wiser.

After we ate and cleaned up, she turned the TV from the news (which hadn't told us anything authentic or newsworthy anyway) to a station that played old country and western music. A female crooner sang passionately about heartbreak to a twangy electric guitar accompaniment. Janet brought out a giant bowl of our beans, and a giant empty melamine bowl.

"Okay. I went ahead and washed all the beans. Now you gotta snap 'em." She demonstrated how to snap both ends off each bean, then snap the bean into inch-long pieces, to fit the jar better. She tossed the scraps into the melamine bowl. We each grabbed a bean and started to snap.

"Before I forget, we'll need this," Janet said, then disappeared into the kitchen. She returned a moment later with a handful of cans of cold beer, and handed them out to us. I didn't recognize the brand. It looked like a generic knockoff of the cheapest beer I'd ever tried in college, and was surprised such a thing existed. I looked over to Twinkie, who was grinning back at me.

"I've been picking beans with Aunt Janet since I was a kid," she said. "This is totally part of the tradition."

We toasted Aunt Janet and her bountiful harvest with our aluminum cans and went to work. The next ninety minutes passed fairly quickly, thanks to the beer and listening to Twinkie and her aunt trading family gossip and old stories. What cracked me up was, by Aunt Janet's second beer, she was grinning, laughing easily, and peppering her tales with curse words (though never the F-word, "because that is never something a lady should say.") There she was, a little old lady with carefully coiffed hair and a prim, floral-print house dress, laughing it up with a brewski. I could see her being the life of the party back in the day.

During a lull in the conversation, I found a moment to ask Janet about her garden, wondering if she could provide some insight on her techniques versus Nicole's.

"So, Janet. I noticed your garden is planned out differently from ours."

"Oh yeah? What'd you do to it?"

"Well, we adopted a combination of square foot, biodynamic, and biointensive, with a few Native American techniques mixed in."

"I ain't never heard of any of that. We just do it the regular way."

"What's that?"

"The regular way. You know, the way everybody does it."

Well, there goes that conversation. I smiled and let the others change the subject.

I was glad for the distraction, because by then, even though the beans were cute and made a satisfying *click* when you snapped them, by then I was sick to death of them. I felt like they would never be done. But we four plowed through the mountain of beans.

Meanwhile, Janet had boiled a big kettle of water, and a smaller kettle of lid pieces. She dumped a bowl of green beans into the water, then a few minutes later scooped them out into prepared mason jars. She then filled the jars with the green bean water, instructed us to add a teaspoon of salt to each jar, then to screw on the lids, fresh from their boiling water, using a dish towel to shield our hands from their heat. Next, she had us arrange the green bean jars into a large pressure cooker. She set the pressure on the cooker, then set a little wind-up timer shaped like a green pepper on her countertop.

"These will be done in about 20 minutes," she explained. "Let the canner cool by itself, until the pressure is gone. You pull 'em out with these tongs," she raised them to show us, "then let 'em finish cooling on the counter. When they're done, just keep 'em away from too much heat or light. They'll last forever."

For the next half hour, she told us all about different techniques that we'd use for different vegetables and fruits, like the tomatoes. I was amazed at how complicated the process was from a chemistry standpoint, but how organically she knew it. My canning book always referred to specific pH and temperatures. She just knew to add a pinch of salt to this vegetable, a dash of spices to that one, and cook times. She never even heard of the term "pH" before, but she knew the concept well enough to shoot down my idea for canning homemade tomato salsa. "You're adding something less acidic than tomatoes," she said. "That'll throw the whole thing off. If you don't have a specific recipe, it's best not to mix ingredients." I wrote down everything she told us on a little note pad, to compare to my reference books later.

Finally, Janet pulled the first batch of jars out of the pressure cooker. She wrapped them loosely in kitchen towels and handed them to us.

"Here, you take the first couple of jars, and go on home. It'll take another day or two to finish canning all these beans. Thank you for helping me get the beans ready." She also handed Twinkie an ice cream bucket full of ripe tomatoes.

"Here, take these too. We got a good crop this year, I can't get rid of 'em fast enough. Are you planting tomatoes too?"

"Yes, ma'am," Twinkie replied. "We just planted them late in the season, you know."

"Well, you can't go wrong with tomatoes," she said. "Come and get some more in a day or two, just pick 'em right off the vine. You don't have to ask. I'll call you girls back to learn how to do the tomatoes. It ain't much different."

"Thank you, Aunt Janet!" we all said, and hugged her goodbye. She saw us out, cracking another can of beer open to sip as she walked us walk away.

When we were beyond earshot, I jabbed Twinkie with my elbow.

"She's a trip, Twinkie."

"Twinkie grinned. "I love my aunt Janet."

"I never would have guessed a genteel lady would knock back beer like that, let alone cuss like a sailor."

"Yeah," Twinkie agreed. "I always wanted to liquor her up and put her on YouTube, showing us how to cook homestyle food. I tried to do it once. Brought a bottle of maple bourbon and my camera to her house and asked her to show me how to cook a sugar cream pie. But she said, 'I can't tell you how! I don't measure shit! I just know how to do it!' I tried showing her YouTube videos, but she said they looked terrible, and said nobody would want to watch an old woman baking a pie. So we just ended up drinking the bourbon and eating pie."

"That's too bad, I bet she'd be a hit."

"Yeah."

I smelled the tomatoes. They smelled like flowers and sunshine. I pulled one out of the basket and bit into it. It was like nothing I'd ever tasted. So sweet and so savory, it took my breath away. I ate that tomato like an apple, wiping the juice off my chin with my forearm like a little kid.

Then I looked down at my clothes. I was filthy, dirt ground into my knees, twigs stuck into my socks, tomato juice dribbles down the front of my shirt. I could only imagine what my hair looked like.

Suddenly I was struck with a dual revelation. First, that was probably the least pretty I've looked in a long time. Second, it didn't matter. I didn't care. I was too busy living.

12

Staring Down Bin Laden

A couple of days later, (it must have been the weekend, not like we're keeping track), Stephanie and I met Jack at his bigger, newer barn. I was trying not to be nervous about it. I knew I was lying when I said I had no problem with hunting, guns, or gross things, but I wasn't sure which of those things would give me away as a liar.

We met him at his barn, the big front door open as usual. He was sitting just inside the door, putting tools into a backpack. We greeted each other, then he led us to his work area, where two rifles laid across the table.

"I bet you thought you'd be hunting today," he said plainly, and fiddled with his ball cap. "Well, if you're gonna hunt, you'll be using a firearm. And if you use a firearm, you need to know how it works and how to take care of it, from top to bottom. We're gonna take these apart, clean them, then put them back together. Then we'll go to my range and try them out. And then, you're gonna take 'em apart and clean 'em again. Repetition, that's how you learn."

My first instinct was relief from the pressure to show nonchalance at killing animals then touching them, only to be replaced by an unexpected dread at having to memorize these contraptions inside and out. I've always been better at book learning than mechanical learning. My brain and mouth locked up, but Stephanie voiced agreement for both of us.

"All right. Let's do it."

"First, before we do anything else, let me show you how to handle a firearm. You NEVER put your finger on the trigger until you are ready to shoot. And you NEVER point your firearm at anything unless you intend to shoot it. And you NEVER shoot something unless you intend to kill it."

We were quiet and still in response. His words were so definite. Black and white. No room for waffling. I felt like we were being indoctrinated into a very serious club. Jack sounded so knowledgeable and commanding, I was seriously impressed. I didn't think he was stupid or weak or anything before, but the change in his demeanor and attitude even had us standing up straighter, completely at attention.

He handed us each a rifle, first demonstrating that it was completely unloaded. He said that was proper gun etiquette; we should learn proper gun etiquette like our life depended on it. I couldn't help but realize people on TV never follow proper gun etiquette. (Yet another example of real-life knowledge ruining otherwise good TV, because if I ever see that happen on TV again, I'll mentally criticize their inaccuracy instead of just enjoying the story.)

Next, he motioned for us to follow him out to his picnic table. Once there, he laid out an old vinyl red gingham tablecloth across the top, then set out an assortment of spray cans, rags, and tools from his backpack.

First, he showed us how to check if the rifle was loaded.

"You showed us already," I said.

"Yeah. And you check it again. It don't matter what anybody tells you, you always check it." Again, he sounded dead serious. He showed us how to pull the bolt handle back to see if a bullet was sitting inside the chamber. With these, we could peer in to see all the way through it to the grass at our feet. There was no way of mistaking whether it was loaded. I liked that. I liked moving the bolt handle back and forth too. It felt official.

Next, he talked us through taking a few parts off to clean them. We popped the bolt off with a little lever to expose the closer end of the barrel, then took Jack's long cleaning rod (first with little pads, then with a pipe cleaner type brush) to dip in a solvent and poke through from the close end of the barrel to the other end.

"No stopping halfway through. When you do anything with a firearm, you decide whether to do it, then you do it. Don't hesitate once you make your decision."

I realized at that moment, because he kept emphasizing the opposite, how pervasive hesitation is in my life. It wouldn't occur to me NOT to hesitate. Especially with a gun in my hand. I looked over at Stephanie. She would never hesitate, I thought, and that's what I admired about her. I started to drift off in thought, but noticed Jack was talking again, so I snapped back.

"Now, these I had already cleaned, so you won't see much. But you'll be surprised how grimy these get after you shoot them. When they get grimy and you don't clean 'em, you risk ruining your firearm. So clean them after every session."

Next, he showed us to clean the bolt and the receiver (If you want to learn more, go find my cheat sheet) while the barrel was soaking in the solvent. Finally, we used the rod to push more unsoaked little cleaning pads back and forth through the barrel until they came out spotless. Our rifles weren't technically dirty, but he had oiled them for long-term storage, so we were essentially removing the protective oil coat.

"That was a lot easier than I expected," I said with happy relief.

"These rifles are pretty easy," Jack agreed. "Semi-automatics and pistols are a bit more complicated, because they have several more parts to disassemble."

At that point, he hoisted up his rifle, which initially looked like ours, because my eyes were so ignorant. Then in a flurry of clicks and cachunks, he stripped his rifle. Piece after piece he pulled off and laid them on the picnic table. So many of them were nested inside each other, it looked like he would never run out of pieces. In the same amount of time it took us to check our rifles for loaded bullets and remove the bolt, he had disassembled his gun (a Beretta semi auto, he called it). A few minutes later, his gun was also clean and reassembled. When he was done, I noticed how much sleeker his gun was than ours, how his didn't have a bolt handle sticking out of it. But the number of pieces to reassemble intimidated me.

Not to Stephanie.

"COOL! Can I try that one too?" She asked.

"Yeah, you can try it, but I'm not gonna let you take it out unsupervised, at least not yet." Jack answered. "It's one of my favorites."

"Fair enough," Steph nodded.

With that done, we followed Jack to his range, which was a straight clearing with a table for us at one end, and a target about 75 yards away at the other end. He walked over to the target block to tack up some paper targets, then returned to us. He pulled a couple of boxes of ammo out of his backpack and put them on the bench in front of us. I strained to see what was printed on the targets, because they didn't look like the concentric circles I expected. Then I recognized them.

"Are those... Osama Bin Laden heads we're shooting at?" I asked.

"Yep. Bought 'em at a gun show. Only got a couple of 'em left."

Stephanie chuckled quietly. I was slightly horrified to aim at a human face smiling back at me, no matter what that face represented, but kept it to myself.

Jack gave us each a pair of ear cups. We tried them on to adjust their fit, then slid them down around our necks so we could hear him. Finally, he showed us how to load our weapons: point them down and away, pull open the breech with the bolt, pop in the ammo, push the bolt forward to close it. He showed us how to flip the safety, then to use the scope to aim at our respective target. Then came the most surprising part of the whole thing.

"Now, don't forget to breathe properly."

He told us to inhale, exhale halfway, hold our breaths, then squeeze the trigger.

I don't know why that reminded me of Nicole's yoga, but it did. It fascinated me so much that two such diametrically opposed activities would both focus on the breath, I closed my eyes and imagined seeing scruffy, bearded, flannel-wearing hunters out in the woods, meditating aloud before firing on a deer: "Center yourself, focus on your breath... Namaste, bitches! KABLOW!"

BOOM!

Stephanie had just fired her first shot at her target. I nearly jumped out of my flesh, so startled by the interruption from my daydream. Jack had apparently been showing her how to hold the rifle and aim while I wasn't paying attention. It was also painfully loud because I forgot to put my ear cups on. Ears ringing, I reeled for a second, positioned my ear cups as fast as I could, then let out a big sigh of relief.

Stephanie emptied her magazine after taking tidbits of advice from Jack in between shots. You could see the enthusiasm in her stance and hear it in her voice. As soon as she was done, we removed our ear cups.

"Oh, that was awesome! I want to go see how I did!"

"Not yet, let us each finish ours before we go down there," Jack replied. "You can look through my scope to see how you did. It's your turn, Emily."

Stephanie's enthusiasm was infectious, I must admit. By now I was more excited than scared. Jack coached me to an optimum foot position and how to hold the rifle, reminded me how to breathe, and pointed out which target was mine to aim at. I held the rifle up close to my face.

"Not right on it, or you could get a hell of a black eye."

"Oh, okay."

"Rest the butt plate into your shoulder. That'll keep it from kicking too far back into your face. And now you can see through the scope easier too."

It just took a moment to found the comfortable way to hold it. I slid my ear cups on and re-discovered my target.

Inhale, exhale, hold, squeeze.

BOOM!

I was immediately surprised both by how hard it impacted my shoulder, and by how little the rifle actually kicked, even counting that I didn't know what to expect. I felt confident that the recoil, something I was initially kind of worried about, wasn't going to bother me at all in the long run.

It felt so powerful. So definite. But so much like a game. I finished my magazine with a calm excitement buzzing inside. Finally, it was Jack's turn. He fired his rounds into the last target smoothly. We walked together to the targets to replace them. Once we were close, I could see the familiar concentric circles emanating from between Bin Laden's eyes.

"Ah, I got a bullseye!" I crowed.

"No, that wasn't yours," Jack corrected. "That was Stephanie's shot. She missed her target entirely and hit your target in the bullseye."

"Ha ha! I got the bullseye!" Steph crowed, grinning from ear to ear. "In your face!"

Jack laughed. "You can't call it yours if you weren't aiming for that target!"

"I don't think that'll stop her from bragging about it anyway," I said with a grin.

We took turns at firing two more magazines' worth before heading back to the picnic table to clean our rifles again. Stephanie and I helped Jack pack everything back up and carry it into his workshop. He told us he'd take us out rabbit hunting next week, and to the feed store the next day to set us up with some chickens. We exchanged thanks and goodbyes, then walked back to the campsite.

"That was fucking awesome," Stephanie said. "I am looking forward to the next time we do that."

"I'm surprised, but I really liked it too," I agreed.

"You're gonna be shooting at rabbits next, not Osama Bin Laden," she reminded me. "You didn't even want to do that."

I shrugged. "We'll see next week."

12

Sting and Bite

As promised, the next day, Jack and Janet led Maggie and Nicole to the rural supply store to buy supplies to keep our own chickens. Hours later, they returned in a caravan loaded with lumber and a bag of hardware, chicken wire, feed, nest boxes, a water dispenser, "scratch," "grit," a couple of cardboard boxes with air holes full of chickens, and a dozen eggs.

"Hey," Stephanie tapped at the eggs. "I thought we were skipping the middleman." She picked one up and shook it a bit.

"We are – hey, careful!" Maggie answered. "Those are unhatched chicks."

"Really," Stephanie said dramatically. She stopped shaking the egg.

"Yep. I'm going to raise them myself."

Stephanie looked at Maggie, eyebrows raised, then returned the egg to its carton. She leaned in close to it.

"SORRY, BABY CHICKIES," she yelled at them.

"Steph, get away from my babies."

Stephanie backed away obediently.

"We're gonna need to build a coop, like, today," Nicole said to Katie. "Can you help us?"

"Of course," Katie answered. She walked over to Jack's truck and peered into the bed to see the materials she had to work with.

"If you build it like mine, your chickens will be safe from foxes and whatnot," Jack advised her. "Go on over to my yard to see for yourself. If you have any questions, just come find me."

"Sure, thanks," Katie answered. She grabbed a notebook and pencil from the pole barn, then left for Jack's back yard.

"So... foxes," I inquired.

"You have to watch out for foxes and other predators," Aunt Janet explained. "Your chickens are tasty, defenseless little shits out here. You don't think you have any foxes around here? Wait 'til you put these chickens out. They'll come out of nowhere and tear up your whole flock in one night."

"Jeez."

"So you make yourself a coop and lock them in at night. You'll want to keep them in your pole barn until you finish the coop. And you might want to get yourself a guard dog. He won't exactly guard the chickens with his life, but he'll get any foxes that come around the coop."

Maggie's eyes lit up at the idea of getting yet another animal, but I was quietly reeling. How many animals do we need to be by ourselves? This seemed like way too much nature, too many mouths to feed, for me all of a sudden.

Aunt Janet spoke out. "Look, it don't matter how you choose to do it, build a coop like Fort Knox, or get a guard dog, or guard 'em yourself with a BB gun all day. But if you want your hens to survive the week, you'll need to come up with a plan to handle predators."

"Oh, we will," said Maggie. "We'll take good care of them." She lifted her carton of eggs to her face and kissed them each in turn with a serene smile on her face.

Stephanie eyerolled and sighed. "I'm gonna help Katie then. We have an impenetrable chicken fortress to build." She reached into the truck bed to unload the supplies.

Jack turned to Maggie. "Y'all already have hay up in your loft, and you can borrow the heat lamp for the chicks. You should be set after that. If you need to borrow any tools, just stop by." He helped Stephanie unload his truck and tipped his hat to the women. Maggie jumped into the truck bed to get a quick ride to the house.

Katie and Maggie returned shortly thereafter with a heat lamp and extension cord, and hand-drawn design diagram for the chicken coop. I looked over the coop diagram. It was so concise and well-drawn in 3-D. She included lumber dimensions, and even how the joints were constructed.

"I want to check the internet to see if there's a newer way to do this," Katie said quietly to me. So I ran into the pole barn to dig out my phone, which I'd more or less given up on using. Turned it on, and after a moment, saw a string of text notifications from Shelby, each a couple of days apart.

SHELBY

Hey I got Katie's note, glad she's OK

SHELBY

Hey are you mad at me? You guys OK?

SHELBY

Text me if you get this. Cell service jacked

SHELBY

Not sure this is gonna work out, can I stay with you

Jarred and excited by the discovery, I cried out about the internet access. Breanna, curled up in the lawn chair in front of the console, jerked her head to stare at me, then jumped up and scurried to her and Maggie's corner. I watched her stretch out on the bed with her phone, the screen illuminating her face.

I ran back out to Katie and showed her.

"We have internet?" she asked excitedly.

"Yeah! And look… Shelby's been trying to text us. She might come stay with us!"

Katie didn't reply to that, but took my phone and opened the browser to review chicken coop designs. While she was busy, I paused to think about the implications of Shelby coming to stay with us. Things were different the last time we invited her. Back then, we weren't concerned with how much food we had. And maybe it was because chickens had been on my mind all afternoon, but it reminded me of the old fable where the chicken spent all summer plowing, growing grain, harvesting, milling, and baking bread, her barnyard friends rejecting her requests for help at every step, only to show up at the end to help her eat the bread. The idea that one of my friends would do that to us made me feel a bit ill. I looked over at Katie, wondering if that's what she was thinking too. She still seemed absorbed in the reference material.

"Okay. I want to modify Jack's design to make our coop portable. That way we can move it every couple of days to keep the ground clean."

"Makes sense to me. Can we keep predators out of it?"

"It says we can."

"Okay. Hey, I forgot to text Shelby back."

Katie looked at me for a moment. "How about you wait until we tell the others?" she said simply. Then she handed me my phone. So maybe she was thinking what I was thinking.

"Okay," I said, taking the phone.

"I'll use mine to download the coop plans," she said, and walked away.

We talked about Shelby's return over dinner. I had my misgivings, and it seemed like Katie did too, but neither of us argued against it. Meanwhile, Maggie and Twinkie were enthusiastic about making room for her, and Breanna also expressed interest. Stephanie didn't say anything either way, but I could tell by how often she crept off to her corner with her cup, she was quietly getting hammered.

Once we decided as a group to re-invite Shelby to our campsite, I texted her. We continued to chat pleasantries about the events of the day while I waited for her to reply, but no reply arrived. It was about 6:00 pm when we heard Breanna yell "No!!" from the back corner. I checked my phone.

"Well. Internet's down again."

"Glad I copied those plans onto paper then," Katie sighed. "Hey Steph, let's finish this coop before it gets dark…." She looked around, but Stephanie was gone. "You guys know where she went?"

"I think she's lying down," I said blandly. "I'll help you finish it."

So Katie and Breanna and I spent the rest of our daylight constructing the chicken coop. It looked like a regular chicken coop, but it didn't have a floor to it, and it was lightweight enough that two of us could lift and reposition it elsewhere on the property. One thing we didn't account for, however, was that the ground wasn't perfectly even, which left a few shallow gaps between the bottom edge of the coop and the ground.

"Do you think that's gonna be a problem?" I asked, pointing them out.

"Nah," Katie guessed. Those gaps are too small for the chickens to get through, and the coop is too heavy for a critter to lift."

I agreed. We called out Maggie and Nicole to inspect our creation, and to help install the chickens, who had been fussing all evening in the cardboard boxes, crazy to get out. Breanna filled their food trough, water dispenser, and nesting boxes, then released them into the coop. They squawked and ran around—well, like chickens-- for a while, then found what they needed and settled down.

I snuck away while Katie, Nicole, Breanna and Maggie focused on the new addition to our campsite, to see how Stephanie was doing. She wasn't in her hammock like I'd guessed earlier. Racking my brain for other places to look, I wandered outside and up the driveway a bit, to a clearing where I knew sometimes she snuck off for peace and quiet. There she was, laying on her back in the grass, staring up at the sky.

"Hey, Steph."

"Hey."

I sat down next to her.

"Are you okay?"

"Yeah. No. Doesn't matter."

"What's going on?" I asked.

She sighed heavily, raised her empty cup, then lowered it again. "Sometimes there's not enough alcohol in the world to exterminate all rational thought."

"Why do you want to do that so badly?"

"Because I don't like it," she said matter-of-factly.

"You don't like what, rational thought?" I asked. "I thought that's your favorite thing."

"No. I don't like being responsible for so many people. I never thought I'd ever get married, or have kids, or even take care of my parents when they got old. Thank god they died before they found out I was gonna ditch 'em in a nursing home. I never even had a fucking pet. Too much responsibility."

"Stephanie, you're not an irresponsible person."

"That's because I try never to bite off more than I can chew. Except now I have."

"You haven't done that here. You're not responsible for all of us."

"Yeah I am! Duh! I have to go out and kill things and rip their guts out, and chop them into pieces.... and then I'll have blood and guts stuck under my fingernails, and that is so gross... and if I don't, we won't have enough to eat."

"You're not responsible for all of that yourself," I replied. "We'll both be doing it. You and me together. You're not responsible for all of us. Just your share of a list of chores we keep as a group, and that's all. WE bring home a couple of deer, and that's all. Maggie and Nicole will be keeping the chickens—"

"Yeah, and who do you think is going to be the one to snap their little necks when it's time to eat one?"

I sat there silently, no answer for her because I hadn't foreseen that circumstance. She was right, though. Most likely, both Maggie and Nicole would declare with great drama and emotion a complete inability to do the deed, then look to Stephanie to close the deal.

"Let's figure that out later," I finally replied. "Who knows, maybe Nicole will go back to being so grossed out by the chickens, she'll be glad to take one out occasionally."

"Ha ha ha! 'Take that, asshole chicken. With my yoga chicken finishing move.'" Stephanie mimicked Nicole, and pantomimed kung fu hand chops to an imaginary bird. She chuckled one more time, checked her empty cup one more time for liquor with a loud, empty slurp, then set it down again.

"Stephanie, I think you've been drinking too much."

"That I would have to agree with you. Because now I am out, and I drank the rest of the camp stash too. But Twinkie helped."

"Well, and I helped too, but you have been drinking lately like your life depended on it. Or so it looks."

She stared up at the sky, pooched her lips out, and breathed kinda loudly, I guessed deep in thought.

"Sometimes I get tired of living in my skin. Drinking fixes it."

"Drinking probably starts it, too."

"Yeah. Vicious cycle. I know it."

"I'm sorry I don't have an answer for you," I said.

"I'm not asking for one."

Then she sat up.

"Uh, I feel like shit now," she mumbled.

"Are you gonna throw up?" I asked.

"Nah. Vomiting is for amateurs. Help me up."

She wasn't too wobbly upon standing, but I helped her back to the campsite. She drank a ton of water at the pump, then walked gingerly to her hammock and passed out. I was tired but too wired from the evening's events to sleep, so I crawled into my hammock to read for a while.

Suddenly I heard shrieks coming from outside. I fell out of my hammock and ran outside to see the pale chickens bouncing off the walls inside the coop, squawking and screaming like crazy. Something was in there with them, but I couldn't see it.

I started yelling and kicking the walls of the coop, which only increased the pandemonium inside it. Lifted one end a bit, hoping only the fox or whatever would escape but the birds would stay inside. Lifted it higher. The fox scampered out, chicken still in his maw, and fled into the forest. A couple of distressed chickens spilled out into the yard as well, though they were drastically less coordinated and rational. I lowered the coop, then tried to recapture the chickens, scurrying and lunging with no success.

Maggie and Breanna suddenly appeared behind me.

"Stop."

Panting, I stood up and looked at Breanna.

"First, let's get the dead one out of there."

I looked inside the coop, and sure enough, one of the birds was laying awkwardly on its side, surrounded by loose feathers. She ducked down into the coop and pulled it out calmly.

"How are we gonna put them back?" I asked.

Breanna spoke up. "Let them calm down. They'll go home on their own."

She propped open the door to the coop, then slowly, gently, shepherded the chickens around it. One by one, they found the door and trotted inside, back into their nesting boxes, and quieted down. She closed the door.

I walked around the perimeter of the coop with my flashlight and found one of the gaps we ignored earlier had been dug larger by the fox. We gingerly shifted the coop away from the fox's hole.

"We're gonna have to figure out how to stop that," I said tiredly.

"Yeah. We'll do it in the morning," Breanna replied.

"Should we bring them into the pole barn tonight?" I asked.

"No. I'll stay out here with them. They're my responsibility." She asked Maggie to stand guard for a moment, then came out with a blanket, pillow, and broom. Breanna nestled herself on the ground facing the coop, broom lying in front of her, ready to wake up and whack at any threats through the night. Maggie tucked her in, then we crept back into the pole barn.

It occurred to me then, we traded soft comfy beds in apartments with well-stocked fridges, for sleeping on the ground to guard our food against predators. There are predators everywhere, of course. The longer we'd been out on our own, the more our old life seemed like an illusion crafted by predators. The predators out here seemed much easier to deal with.

13

Gift Horses

The next morning, Maggie and Katie left for the rural supply store in Maggie's SUV. Their mission was to secure the coop enough that Maggie wouldn't have to babysit it with a broom every night. We also decided to replace the two dead birds, even though Maggie had a batch of eggs due to hatch within the next day or so.

What they came back with, however, will shock you! (Just kidding.)

With GPS still unavailable, they had to navigate by Maggie's recollection of where the store was. She guessed incorrectly at an intersection, and ended up driving past a landmark that convinced her she'd made a wrong turn.

It looked like a prison.

Out in the middle of nowhere, off a rural county road. It was still under construction, but a tall chain link fence with razor or barbed wire already lined the perimeter. The shell was completed, but its few windows were not yet installed. It was tall, sprawling, dreadfully gray. It instantly chilled Maggie and Katie to see it. Our city already had a jail; our county already had a detention facility. What was the purpose of this prison, and who was building it?

"Well…. Did you read the signs on the fence?" I asked, interrupting their tale. "Usually they advertise the construction company."

"No, I forgot to pay attention. I'm sorry," Maggie answered sheepishly. Katie shook her head.

"Maybe it's not a prison," I argued. "Maybe it's just a factory."

"With razor wire?" Katie scoffed. "Out in the middle of nowhere?"

I shrugged. "Maybe they're afraid of foxes."

Katie shrugged.

"By the looks of it, they're working overtime to finish it. There were so many workers on the site, it looked like an anthill."

"Hm. Well, glad you found the supply store. Where is it? Will you write out directions so we have it in the future?"

"Sure." Maggie jotted down the location of the store while Katie commenced the coop upgrade.

Later that afternoon, Shelby arrived.

As always, she was impeccably dressed for the occasion, with designer weather-proof boots, crisp safari shorts and top, a tidy silver bracelet, really cute sunglasses, and a hat to protect her head from harmful UV rays. She looked dressed to wrestle alligators on TV. We greeted her at her car. I noticed her car was full of luggage, but didn't see much food. My heart sank a bit.

As usual, Stephanie said aloud what I was thinking.

"Were you planning on chipping in, or are you just visiting?"

"Oh yeah, I'm chipping in," she said with sly grin. She swung her purse around and whipped out the biggest wad of cash I'd ever seen in person. We were all taken aback. Steph laughed.

"What'd you do, hold up a bank?"

"Nah. The price of gold is crazy high these days. I just sold some of my jewelry."

"Wow."

"I didn't buy anything because I didn't know what you guys needed. So here you go." She handed the cash to Twinkie. Twinkie flipped through the bills, eyes wide. Shelby then reached into her passenger side and handed me a city newspaper, dated today.

"Holy shit, Shelby. There's gotta be a couple grand in here."

"At least four. That oughta buy us some nachos and margaritas, right?"

We cheered and a couple of us group hugged her, then helped her carry her stuff in. There wasn't enough canvas to make a compartment for her, so Stephanie volunteered to move up to the hay loft for Shelby to take her corner.

For the next hour or two, we helped Shelby settle in, and caught up on each other's news. We also wanted to know why she decided to move in with us. I was trying to listen and browse through the newspaper at the same time.

"We didn't think you'd make the jump here, honestly," Twinkie said, carrying a box of Stephanie's stuff to the hay loft ladder.

"Well, yeah," Shelby responded. "I didn't have any interest in it until recently. But shit out there is just getting too unreal."

"You mean, with the raids on the projects?" Katie asked.

"Didn't you hear?" Shelby replied. "Your neighborhood is gone already. They were bulldozed almost immediately. Now someone's putting up condos already, upscale, with shopping on street level. You know, wine bar, tapas. Oh, and rumor has it, a Cheesecake Factory. Walls are going up now. Looks nice."

"But wait," Katie said. "Our water was bad. City council wasn't going to repair the pipes anytime soon."

Shelby shrugged. "I guess they changed their minds."

Stephanie climbed back down the ladder and gestured to Twinkie to hand her a bag of her stuff. "But that neighborhood was full of people. Where'd they go?"

"I don't know. They were probably all criminals and aliens and welfare cheats anyway," Shelby commented.

Twinkie and Katie both stopped in their tracks to glare at her.

"That's what everyone else tells me. I'm just telling you."

"Jeez, Shelby."

"That's fucking horrible."

"It wasn't my idea, okay? Like I said, shit's just getting too unreal."

"Hey…" I interrupted, alarmed at what I'd just read. "What's this about schools being closed?"

"What?" Stephanie was halfway up the ladder, frozen in place.

"Yeah. Public schools are now closed. Done." Shelby hoisted a suitcase into the corner, then returned to us.

"Wait. What?"

"They can't do that!" Nicole cried out.

"They did."

"Why?"

"According to my friends, the school system was a waste of taxpayer money, what with Common Core and all that standardized testing, and teachers were getting too radical, so they decided to shut them down altogether."

"Well, yeah, the system seemed pretty jacked, but isn't that like throwing the baby out with the bath water?" I commented.

Shelby shrugged.

"What do they mean, getting too radical?" Katie asked.

"Yeah. You know, all that bullshit about sex education, climate change, revisionist liberal history, trying to keep God out of schools."

"That's not bullshit," Stephanie argued.

"Well, the government tried to clamp down on all that, but so many teachers refused to stop teaching it, they just shut the entire public school system down."

"What are kids doing then?!"

"Oh, home school. Online. That's messing with a lot of my boy friends with kids, you know."

"Ugh. I don't like hearing about your affairs," Maggie cringed.

Shelby shrugged. "It's not like I'm going into details."

"What about college?" Nicole asked. "I was going to a state school."

"Closed."

"What the hell!" Nicole stomped her feet and looked ready to start kicking something.

"Hey, watch the luggage," Shelby cautioned her.

"How am I gonna finish my degree now?" Nicole cried out.

Meanwhile, I had finished browsing the newspaper, and folded it back up. "Do you know how we can get the real news?" I asked. "It's all either generically pro-government, or replaced by sitcom reruns. Even the internet seems like it's been gutted, and that's if we can even log on to it."

"Don't know… I never watched the news before. But a lot of my friends have given up on social media."

"Given up or been kicked off?" Stephanie asked.

"I don't know. It's not like I talk to them in real life."

"That reminds me," Stephanie said. "A couple of weeks ago, we tried to get into the city, but cops set up a roadblock and wouldn't let us pass. Is that all done now?"

"Not exactly," Shelby replied. There are checkpoints set up at random places in town to check for citizenship status. If you're white like me, they won't even bother to check you. But if you're not white and you don't have your driver's license on you, you're fucked. Away you go. And I heard sometimes, they'll call your license fake and take you into custody anyway. One of my friends was threatened with that at a checkpoint. He said he only got away because he still had the DMV receipt in his car."

"Jeez."

But anyway, the worst thing I've seen is the catcalls I get out in public," Shelby continued. "You know. Guys on the street used to see me and go, 'Hey baby, you're looking fine,' or 'Hey, what's your name?' Now these assholes are out there in packs, yelling 'Come here, bitch, I want to talk to you.' Or 'What, you a little snowflake, bitch? You need a real man!'" Shelby pantomimed strutting and obscene hand gestures with a cruel, gravelly voice. "And that freaks me out. I don't feel safe anymore, even with all the extra cops driving around."

"Well, we're glad you're here," Twinkie said. We all nodded in agreement. Snickers padded over to Shelby and rubbed her face on her boot.

"Thanks for having me." She reached down to scratch Snickers behind her ears. Snickers craned her head upward for more.

"Excuse me," Maggie suddenly appeared next to Shelby, grabbed her cat, and walked away to her compartment.

Shelby sighed. "I think I pissed her off."

She followed Maggie behind the canvas partition.

We continued to shuffle belongings around, while the two spoke quietly. But after just a moment, their voices were loud enough that we could hear every word.

"I don't even want your money. How could you even do such a thing?" Maggie's voice was a shrill almost-whisper. "You're like a prostitute!"

"I am not a prostitute!" Shelby countered indignantly.

"Then explain all that jewelry you sold. Guys didn't give it to you because they loved you."

"Maggie. You're right. Guys didn't give me jewelry because they love me. And they didn't give it to me for sex. They did it to impress people. And not even to impress me, they did it to impress anybody who knows they did it. They do it because it makes THEM feel good. I don't even care about the jewelry."

"How could you not care?! What I wouldn't give for one guy to love me enough to give me nice jewelry, and you have a ton of guys lined up and you don't even care. You just fuck 'em and get presents."

"I fuck them because I want to. No strings attached. No payment expected."

"Yeah, right," Maggie said dismissively.

"And who are you to give me a quota?" Shelby argued. "It's my vagina, I get to put whatever I want in it. You don't get to decide that for me. You're just jealous."

At this, Stephanie silently WOWed at us, eyes wide.

"Of course I'm jealous," Maggie said, her voice thick with frustration. "You get guys the time, and I get none, no matter what."

"Sweetie," Shelby cooed. "Like I said. They don't love me. None of them do. And that's fine. If you want to get laid, I can get you laid. But that's not what you're after. And if you want nice jewelry, buy it yourself. Don't sit around hoping a boyfriend will buy it for you. That's prostitution."

Then they were quiet. Twinkie and I looked at each other for a moment, holding our breath, waiting for the next words.

"Look," Shelby continued, "you want Prince Charming to come sweep you away and take care of you. Fine. I really hope you find him. But I'm not looking for that. I just date and have a good time. Don't call me a prostitute because we go for different things. It's not fair."

"I'm sorry."

"It's okay," Shelby answered. "Hey. I saved something for you…. Here. It's Tiffany. And no, it's not from a guy. My mom bought it for me last Christmas."

"Really?"

"Yeah. Thought you might like it."

"Thanks."

A moment later, Shelby came out of Maggie's compartment, the silver bracelet absent from her wrist. Twinkie motioned her closer, then gave her a hug.

"Sorry she unloaded on you like that," she said quietly. "She's been really stressed out lately."

"I get it," Shelby replied. "Some of us are better at handling chaos than others." She winked at Twinkie.

They walked back to the counter, where Twinkie tapped on the wad of cash. "Thank you so much. We can really put this to good use. We started a garden and raising chickens to be more self-sustainable, but we're gonna need more help. This will go a long way." She looked around at all of us. "We've been throwing a couple ideas around. Let's figure out which ideas we're gonna try, then put together a shopping list."

"I know what we need first!" Twinkie cried. "More electricity! I want a real fridge, and an oven, and--"

"We already decided we can't afford that," Stephanie reminded her.

"We have the money now," Twinkie replied, patting the cash. "To hire an electrician to come out and give us more outlets, more power."

"Uh, you don't want anyone to come out here," Shelby cautioned.

"Why not?"

"Because you're technically harboring 'fugitives,' that's why."

"What are you talking about?" I asked.

"Nobody here is a fugitive," Steph retorted.

"Twinkie is," Shelby said, looking at her sadly.

"She can't be. She's done nothing wrong," I argued.

"She's Muslim."

"She's about as Muslim as I am a Christian! She eats bacon, for god's sake... she drinks vodka... at the same time." Steph exclaimed.

"They don't give you a bacon test before they deport you," Shelby argued.

"Actually, I don't eat bacon." Twinkie interjected.

"You're not helping your case here, Aaliyah," Stephanie muttered.

"Deport her? To where, Indiana? That's her country of origin," I argued.

"Don't ask me, I don't have any answers," Shelby replied, flustered. "This whole thing is stupid. All of it. Just understand. Twinkie is now officially in hiding, and for good reason. We do not want to find out what happens to her if she shows her face in public at this point."

That shut us up for a moment.

"So you believe, that if we call an electrician out here, he'd call the cops on Twinkie? Her?" Stephanie pointed at Twinkie. Twinkie then made a scary bear face and pretended to claw menacingly at us. I couldn't help but laugh at her.

"Yes." Shelby said with a strong note of finality.

"Well, guess you're REALLY not going back to the Kitchen Club Emporium then," I said ruefully to Twinkie. She looked back at me, rolled her eyes, then smiled at me, shaking her head.

Stephanie turned to me. "Speaking of that," she said quietly, "It's time."

I stood up. "Bye guys. Don't let Twinkie eat anybody," I grinned.

I nodded back at Stephanie. We waved goodbye to our friends.

It's time to go hunting with Jack.

14

Pacifist, Hunter

One thing that fascinates me about hunting is how much you try to learn about the lifestyle of the thing you're going to kill. Jack explained morning and late afternoons are the best time to look for rabbits, our first quarry. They'll be out looking for food, as will we. Why rabbits? Everything else is off-season right now, rabbits are easy to handle, and Jack said if you can learn how to hit a rabbit, surely you can hit a deer.

Jack said we were ready for our first hunt. Stephanie said she was ready. I said I was too, but as we picked up our freshly cleaned and loaded rifles, loaded our cargo pockets with tools, and walked single file out into the wilderness, I realized I might not be as ready on the inside as I was on the outside.

Jack led the way into the forest, first along a flat, mowed grassy path wide enough for an ATV, then veering off into the trees where the underbrush allowed us room to move. It looked like Jack had managed to wear down these paths himself over the years, but nature constantly threatened to take them back over. I guessed that if Jack didn't walk this same path every week, it would soon become invisible.

We walked for at least 15 minutes, the sound of the forest filling our ears. The farther we walked, the more aware I became of the sounds we made. We started walking slower, more carefully. Jack quit talking a few minutes before we stopped. He motioned for us to join him on one side of a fallen tree, then spoke to us in a whisper.

"You won't be able to hear them unless they take off. But they're easy enough to see. They don't expect us here, so they'll be out in the open, eating leaves off young shoots between the trees. We can use this tree for cover, and you can rest your rifle on it too, if you want."

We scanned the forest floor for rabbits for a moment, before I spied one under a shrub. He was peacefully munching on the grass and dandelions growing around him.

"Jack, I found one."

"All right, you go first then. You remember what to do?"

"Yes."

I popped in my earplugs, checked my hunting partners to make sure they knew what I was doing, looked around for a reason not to shoot, then flipped my safety off and sighted the rabbit. Then I looked at Jack.

"Aim right for the chest," Jack gestured and mouthed at me.

I stared down the barrel at the rabbit. Inhale, exhale, hold...

I can't do it.

I stopped breathing, moving. I couldn't do it. I just kept watching the rabbit sitting there, ears alert, wondering where the danger is.

I felt movement beside me. Stephanie drew her rifle, aimed, and fired. She let out a wordless yell.

First I couldn't bear to look, then I peeked over. The rabbit lay on its side, one paw up, twitching. I looked away again, woozy.

Stephanie and Jack walked over to it. After a moment, Jack picked it up and brought it to where I was standing. By now, I was reeling from the unreality of it, the limpness of the creature, the casual way he carried it back like a sack of groceries.

But it was groceries.

He complimented Stephanie on her steadiness. I watched numbly as he pointed to the entry wound right in the middle of the rib cage. He said it was a "clean kill."

"Why was it twitching?" Stephanie asked. My stomach rolled over just hearing those words.

"That's just the last muscle impulses working their way through. Muscles finish what they were gonna do even after the animal dies. No, that was quick and painless for the rabbit, and you didn't ruin the meat. Nice job."

I could do nothing but look away and try to breathe.

Jack put the rabbit into a bag and slung it over his shoulder. I followed them as they continued to look for small game. An hour and another rabbit later, this time shot by Jack, we headed back to his barn to clean them.

When we arrived, Stephanie pulled me aside just outside the barn and gave me a serious gaze.

"Do you remember what you promised me?" she asked quietly.

I swallowed and nodded. "Yeah, I do."

"Because it didn't look like you had the stomach to kill anything out there."

"I know."

"And I don't want to have to do all this myself."

"You're not going to."

"I didn't mind pointing the gun and firing. It kind of felt like a video game. But I don't want to touch it. I don't want to think about what it used to be."

We looked at each other for a moment in silence. Her eyes, normally the essence of devil-may-care, betrayed her sadness; through her carefully practiced expression of nonchalance, I could see a plea for help. Suddenly, I felt really sorry for her. She'd just reached the end of her capacity to not give a shit.

I hugged her.

"Go on home, I got this."

She hugged me back, handed me her rifle, then turned to walk back to the campsite without saying a word.

I took a deep breath and turned toward Jack's workshop. Stood up a little straighter. Started whispering to myself, I can do it, if I just do it. Crossed the threshold of his outbuilding and propped the rifles against the wall, letting my eyes adjust to indoor lighting.

He had pulled the rabbits out of the sack and laid them out across the counter next to his big utility sink. Next, he pulled out a knife.

"I'm gonna do the first one, then you're gonna do the second," he said. "It's not hard, but you want to do it right, so you don't ruin the meat and make a mess."

He took the knife, grabbed the fur at the back, then poked the knife through. Poked a couple fingers of each hand inside the fur, then pulled outward, ripping and flipping the fur inside out as it reached either end. A couple of chops at either end, chop chop chop chop, then he set the fur aside.

Suddenly, the carcass was much easier for me to look at it. It looked like a roasting chicken I'd buy at the store, or one of the fetal pigs I had to dissect in school. I remembered the first time I had to deal with those, when my squeamishness disappeared fairly quickly.

"Then you pull out the insides?" I asked.

"Yep."

Of course, they weren't conveniently placed in a plastic bag for me to pull from the neck hole like a grocery store chicken, but they weren't much harder to remove. He finished dressing the rabbit and rinsed it out well in his sink. The whole process took less than five minutes. He laid down the meat on a fresh plastic bag on the counter. It was grayish pink, smooth, clean.

Already, I felt relieved about the experience. It was such a help to see it in later stages, so I could relate it to other things that I'd successfully gained the courage to handle.

It was my turn. I took Jack's knife and went to work. It took me a bit longer because I was afraid to apply too much pressure with the knife, but I did it. A few moments later, my rabbit laid next to his.

He led me into the farmhouse kitchen, where we then used a butcher knife to divide the meat. Butchering was more complicated than dressing, but when it was all done and he laid out the pieces, I was able to see the logic behind each cut. As we butchered our animals, he talked about how each piece could be grilled or stewed. He bagged my rabbit and handed it to me, a smile on his face.

"Just wait 'til you eat it," he said. "It's well worth the effort."

I took a deep breath, smiled back at him, then took the bag.

"Thank you, Jack," I said. He nodded at me.

I walked home, sighing a few times to stretch out the lungs that were cramped tight with anxiety for so much of the day. The sun had ducked behind the taller trees, dappling the light on the road home. I listened to the leaves rustle, the birds sing, my footsteps padding down the worn gravel lane. I was so relieved that I found the courage to do something I was scared of, I felt amazingly alive.

I held up the plastic bag with the rabbit meat to look at it again. It wasn't a rabbit anymore, it was a precious gift; one I could never take for granted, one that I was about to share with my family.

That night we sat around the campfire, cooking my rabbit, each taking a bite because one rabbit doesn't stretch far between eight people (it was delicious), and just hanging out, more or less like we always had. We'd run out of alcohol so we weren't laughing as loud, and the topic of food was more about its being a commodity than a source of amusement. But we were all in good spirits, even Breanna. We reminisced joyously about our carefree days in the past, shared some of our best crazy stories, even if half of us had already heard them before. It was fun to hear them again, to take a break from all the seriousness of what we'd spent our days doing.

And as we talked and laughed, I thought about how kicking back and enjoying each other's company was just as important as the food and the shelter we'd been working on. Like, why bother living if we aren't going to enjoy it?

Eventually though, long after the glow of the campfire replaced the sun, I grew tired of the crowd and needed some quiet and solitude. I said goodnight to my friends and made my way to my compartment. There I found a surprise. She must have done it while I was out hunting. Katie painted a lotus flower on my canvas wall, with delicately streaked big pink petals. For a moment, I flashed back to the rabbit I had skinned earlier in the day. Its flesh, just like the flower, was pink, streaked, soft. But my mind drifted back to the lotus flower, and the kindness behind the brush strokes that created it.

15

Breaking Shells

For another couple of days, we were riding high on satisfaction from the successes of establishing our kick-ass garden, our first successful hunt, four nights without disaster in our chicken coop (we joked about making one of those industrial accident counting signs for it), and the hatching of Maggie's chicks. Maggie's chicks were seriously adorable. Seemed like every few minutes, somebody was over at their pen, smiling and cooing over them. They made just enough noise to be cute, not too much to be obnoxious. So that's why they call those yellow marshmallow candies "Peeps."

But you know how life goes. Nothing ever lasts forever. Especially satisfaction. Especially with us fickle women. Yeah, I said it. Maybe the stereotypes have a grain of truth to them? So our elation faded, replaced by a collective, gnawing desire for things we didn't have.

Stephanie wanted more alcohol, naturally.

Twinkie did too, as soon as she realized Stephanie drank all of the group's stash on top of her own.

And to be honest, I wanted some too. And Shelby and Katie and Nicole. We stopped short of accusing Stephanie of hogging it all, because she looked a bit ashamed anyway.

Now that we had fresh eggs and rabbit and chicken to add to our diets, we wanted spices to cook with, and couldn't wait for our own freshly sprouted herb garden to deliver. Parsley, thyme, bay leaves…. And bacon. We were all (except for Twinkie) craving bacon. At the first mention of it, we started wailing and feigning fainting, and laughing at ourselves.

Twinkie and I figured we'd need more jars to can our vegetables for the winter, so we added it to the list. And Katie wanted some lumber to make another clothesline and a pole for me to dress Stephanie's deer this fall.

Breanna said she had run out of face minerals. I'm not even sure what face minerals are, and she didn't seem to look any different, but there was no reason to argue with her.

Maggie said she was gonna die if she didn't get a pedicure. Breanna seconded that, so they decided to go to town for us and do the shopping.

You could tell by the dreamy, distracted look on Maggie's face that she was itching to go back to town no matter what. The desire seemed to bubble up and boil over after Shelby arrived with that huge wad of cash. Not that Maggie wanted to go on a wild, irresponsible shopping spree – it was more that suddenly, there was a justification to drive to town. Lately, we only had reasons to avoid driving town… you know, if you don't leave your house, you don't spend any money.

Anyway, as soon as we decided that someone should go on a supply run, Maggie and Breanna both volunteered so hard, it seemed ridiculous to contest it. In hindsight, I think it was because they were more attached to the world we'd left behind – TV, shopping malls, mocha lattes. But we trusted Maggie to make decent choices with the money we sent with her, and since she donated the lion's share of the food and the freezer, she well earned her place as an authority of our inventory. Her integrity we did not question.

To be fair, we no longer really questioned Breanna's integrity. After the first month or so, when we discovered some of our worst worries were actually coming to pass, she seemed to commit to our adventure more, just like the rest of us. She did her fair share cultivating our crops with Nicole's guidance. She was a natural at caring for the chicks and the poultry, and nobody had to remind her to do it. At mealtimes, she still didn't talk much, but at least she was sitting and eating with us. She used to hide in her compartment and snack on whatever you could eat one-handed on her inflatable bed.

The fact that Breanna quit hiding from everything and started participating, led Stephanie to lay off the insults, which made the entire situation more pleasant for all of us. Was Breanna turning into one of us? No. But nobody expected her to. Personally, I still felt a bit of sympathy for her. She never would have agreed to join us out there. She never took part in our crazy childhood schemes either. She just didn't have the resources to live without Maggie, even with a job.

So Maggie and Breanna drove off the next morning to go shopping for us, with our blessing to hang out there for a while and enjoy the change of pace; check for better internet service, maybe watch some TV at Twinkie's house (she gave Maggie her key to check on her house anyway).

We expected them to be gone all day.

The shadows of the trees in the late afternoon stretched across the gravel road when I saw Maggie's SUV tear down it at full speed. I was instantly alarmed. Maggie never drives like that.

She didn't park in the parking lot, but skidded to a halt in the lane, leaving skid marks and throwing up dust.

When I saw there was nobody in the passenger seat, my heart stopped. My brain feebly scrambled for a good reason why I was seeing what was in front of me.

Maggie threw her door open, crying, screaming. She stopped to bend over slightly and vomit into the grass. I ran up to her, I don't remember if I was making noise or not. Maybe I was too, because the other girls were upon us in an instant.

I put my hand on Maggie's shoulder as she was still bent over vomiting and said, "Maggie, what, Maggie, what," a bit too loud, but the answer appeared in my head before she had the sense to say it out loud.

"No," I said, my voice trailing off.

"My sister…" Maggie glanced at me like a cornered animal. "MY SISTER!" she wailed, completely beside herself in shock.

"What the holy fuck," Stephanie said, summing up the sentiment for all of us.

"Maggie, what happened?" Twinkie asked, her voice pitched in terror. She'd circled around to flank Maggie, put her arm around her. She and I started to lead Maggie toward the fire pit, at least to give her some distance from her vomit, even if she wasn't ready to talk yet.

"We were…" Maggie gasped out as her legs obeyed Twinkie and me. "These guys…"

"Where's Breanna." Stephanie's voice turned rock hard. It wasn't a question. It sounded more like a threat.

"He killed her!" Maggie wailed.

Our voices joined her wail, a cacophony of useless questions and wordless answers. We clung together beside the fire pit as the world melted away. It was just our bodies, our breath, our sound, and our shock. That moment may as well have been branded into our flesh.

We stayed huddled as Maggie gathered her bearings enough to tell us what happened. She smeared her snot and tears across her face with her forearm and took a deep breath.

"We… we went, to the mall…. We went, to the grocery store, got the food and drinks…. Then we went to the home improvement store to get the stuff Katie asked for…." She coughed and wiped her face again.

"It took us forever to find the stuff on the list, we didn't know where anything was. We walked around the store…. A couple of guys started trying to talk to us, they were offering to help but they seemed so creepy, we told them we were fine…." She started crying again.

"They followed us out to my car and asked us stupid stuff, if we had boyfriends, where we lived…. If we needed help loading my car…. We were doing it already, we didn't need their help, we said no thank you…." She starting sobbing.

Stephanie broke away and started pacing back and forth. The rest of us were frozen in place waiting for the rest of the story. My breath was arrested. Maggie's breath came in heaves.

"Then a big white van pulled up behind my car. We tried to get in my car but those guys grabbed us and the back door of the van opened up and another guy came out and they grabbed her and they-- " she let out a sudden growl of anger – "they dragged her into the back of the van and they just raped her and beat the shit out of her because she was fighting back so hard."

We boiled with fury at this point.

"And I was screaming stop, police, and I tried to pull one of them off her, but he just knocked me off. He said "wait your turn, cunt." Her breath, still heavy, was now forced by rage, not loss.

"My sister bit the one guy's arm, hard enough to make him scream. He picked her up and slammed her head down on this thing, again and again, until she quit moving...."

"Jesus Christ, Maggie...."

"Her face... when I saw it, I knew... When he realized it, that she, they shut the doors and drove away. I don't know where they took her!"

She paused again to weep as we huddled closer to her. Stephanie was still pacing, more frantically.

"And I was just standing there in the parking lot, screaming, and the police showed up..."

"Did you give him descriptions? Of the men, of the van?"

"He didn't care. He asked me what she looked like, and asked me if we were soliciting. I was like, what the fuck question is that? He said this is a known location where guys pick up whores. I said No we're not whores. Then he asked me if they might have been illegals. I told him what they looked like. He didn't even file a report."

"What?!" We all spat out.

"He said she'd probably be home later and just left. There's no way, her head was, her eyes...." She looked up at me with her own bloodshot, puffy eyes. They chilled me to the bone. "There's no way she isn't dead. But they took her, they took her and I don't know where to find her."

"Are you sure she's dead?" Stephanie interjected. She'd stopped pacing and looked ready to pounce.

"Yes…." Maggie cried. "I can't…"

"It's okay," Twinkie spoke as she leaned her cheek into Maggie's hair, trying to comfort her.

"When did this happen?" Stephanie prodded her.

"I don't know, an hour ago?"

Nobody knew what to say after that. For a moment, we were one, a tableau of sisterhood in shock. But those of us more prone to action in crisis each rose to adapt in our own way.

Twinkie looked over to Nicole and nodded at her. Nicole replaced Twinkie as Twinkie broke away long enough to grab a box of tissues and a damp washcloth to wipe the tears gently from Maggie's face. She discreetly wiped her own away with her arm.

Stephanie crouched in front of Maggie.

"Tell me what they looked like. Their van. I'm gonna find them."

"I don't know what else to tell you," she said brokenly.

"Steph," Nicole said gently, silently imploring her to wait.

Steph looked away in frustration, then stood back up to resume her pacing. Suddenly, she turned and headed to Jack's house. I took off to catch up with her determined march.

"Steph, what are you doing?"

"I'm gonna get my fucking gun."

"What?"

"We are never going unprotected ever again."

"Uh, OK." I wasn't really expecting this. I thought she was going say she was calling the police.

"I should have gone with them. Fuck, I should have gone. They can't fucking do anything right," she said, spitting the last words out in frustration.

I looked over at her and saw tears welled up in her eyes.

"Stephanie, you're not blaming them, you're blaming yourself, and that's not fair so just stop it," I said sharply.

"I'm not letting this go," she said just as sharply. She stopped and looked at me. "I'm gonna find 'em, and then I'm gonna fucking kill them." As soon as she said those words, I felt in the pit of my stomach she was completely serious.

"I know." I said it simply. No judgment implied.

We locked eyes, the two of us who had become viscerally acquainted with death not three days ago. She knew better than the others girls what those men had done. And she knew, better than the other girls, how to do the same back to them. In that moment, looking at her, I was seared by the conflict. I didn't want her to lose a part of her humanity by drawing another's man's blood, but honestly, I envied her grit.

All of this passed in a few seconds of our gaze. She turned back toward Jack's house once more.

"How are you gonna find them?" I asked.

"I don't know. Maybe there's a surveillance camera. Find the van. I got a friend at the sheriff's office who can run the make and model for addresses."

"How are you going to get the gun?" I asked, following her.

"I'm not telling them why," she said. "And you're not going to, either."

I stopped in my tracks.

"Steph?" I asked.

She turned around and stared at me.

"What?"

"Good luck," I nodded to her, then turned back toward the campsite.

The situation wasn't much different when I returned. I had to stay busy, away from everybody. I wanted no questions. Nicole and Twinkie eventually coaxed Maggie off the picnic table seat and into the pole barn, each one flanking her in case she collapsed. Shelby tried her best to prepare their way ahead of them, holding the door open, turning on the Christmas lights. Once inside, the new environment surrounded Maggie with a thousand tiny reminders of her sister, which made her start sobbing all over again. They led her to her corner compartment, the one she shared with Breanna. Once there, she fell onto her bed, clinging to it for dear life and weeping. I wondered if their bed still smelled like Breanna. I rejoined the huddle around her bed, unsure of what else to do with myself.

About 10 minutes later, Stephanie returned. I glanced over to see her discreetly carry one of Jack's rifles up to her hayloft. I looked over to Katie, who looked tiredly back at me.

"I'm going to make some dinner," I said hesitantly. "Maybe someone will be hungry soon." Katie and Twinkie looked up and nodded briefly. I leaned over to kiss Maggie on the forehead, then left her crowded compartment for the kitchen to poke through the pantry for comfort food.

I thought I heard the far-off spitting of gravel as if a vehicle was approaching. As I perked my ears to confirm the sound, Stephanie barked out hoarsely in alarm from up in the hayloft.

"Maggie, what color was the van?!"

16

Transformation

"WHAT?!"

Twinkie was the first to react. On her feet in a flash, she leapt up the ladder to Stephanie. Shelby, Katie, and Nicole bounded out of Maggie's compartment and waited breathlessly in the middle of the pole barn for an explanation. Maggie followed them out, looked up at Stephanie with red, swollen eyes.

"White."

"Holy shit," Stephanie erupted, the stress in her voice hitting my chest like a baseball bat. She leaned over the edge of the hayloft. "Lock the doors," she hissed. Katie, Shelby, and Nicole scattered ineffectually in an attempt to obey the command.

"What's happening?!" Shelby asked, panicked.

"I think they're here…" Twinkie whispered down to us loudly, her head peeking out from the edge of the hayloft. She was on her hands and knees, trying not to be seen.

"How can that be?!" I cried.

"How do we lock the big door?!" Nicole squealed. She'd bounced from one side of the door to the other, searching fruitlessly for some sort of lever to pull or knob to twist.

"The padlock in the corner," Katie answered, and raced to where she herself was pointing, at the very front corner of the pole barn. She picked up a big padlock, then attached it to a nearby latch.

Then we noticed the rumble of a vehicle outside, which caused us to all suddenly go silent. Vibrating with panic, we then focused our attention on the small side door. The hardware was antique, with a large, obsolete keyhole under the knob, no deadbolt. Katie and Nicole each leaned against the door, hoping to secure it with body weight and force of will.

We waited for a moment to hear the van's doors open, but heard nothing but its unfamiliar engine idling.

"What are they doing?!" Nicole whispered to us.

"Do we know it's them?" I asked upward toward Steph and Twinkie.

"It's them," Twinkie leaned over the edge and whispered. "They keep looking over at Maggie's SUV and talking to each other."

Maggie let out a weird choking noise.

I looked up at Twinkie and Stephanie. "How would they have known she was here?"

"They must have followed her," Twinkie whispered back before disappearing from view.

"We gotta get help," I replied, eyes wide.

Shelby pulled her phone out of her pocket, the only one of us still in the habit of carrying one, and tapped a few times.

"Hello, yes, I'd like to report, uh, scary people in my driveway…." She paced toward Maggie, standing catatonically in the middle of the pole barn, then hovered there.

"Hold on, let me ask." She looked up at Twinkie helplessly. "She wants to know what they look like."

"Couple of rednecks. Uh, scruffy white guys, beards, ball caps. We can only see two, in the front seats. Skinny guy behind the wheel, plus a beefy guy."

Shelby murmured the description of the driver and passenger into her cell phone.

"No, they aren't Hispanic…. Yeah they did, they killed my friend earlier today! Yeah but they didn't come. No, I wasn't there…. No, they haven't done anything, yet. Please, please come help us. I'm serious." After several seconds, she double checked her phone. "They fucking hung up on me."

"911?!" Katie asked.

"Yeah."

You could hear Stephanie cursing quietly up in the hayloft.

"Jack," I said. "I'll go get him. He can help us."

"How you supposed to do that?" Katie whispered hard. There was only one reasonable way out, and that was through the door they were barricading with their own bodies.

"What else can we do?!" I asked in response.

Then we heard two van doors slam shut.

"What the fuck you want?" Stephanie yelled out. I hoped she was pointing the rifle at them.

"Hey baby, settle down. We're just wondering what you're up to," a male voice said. Maggie started shaking her head, then breathing hard.

"None of your goddamned business," Steph replied.

"I think one of our friends is out here," he said, looking around at our campsite. "in your uh, pole barn. Or whatever you got going on out here. We want to talk to her."

"Nobody in here wants to talk to you."

"Now, how do you know that?" the voice continued. "I didn't see you askin' nobody. Come on, just let us in." We heard footsteps.

"Take one fucking step closer," Stephanie said harshly. Now I know she was pointing her rifle at them. And all I could think was, I gotta get out of here, I've got to get Jack.

"Hey, sweetheart, you don't need that," the voice said. "It's cool. We just came to talk."

Twinkie once again poked her head out toward us to whisper. "There's only two of them so far. They've got their hands up."

That felt like my cue.

"Guys, I need to get out. Let me out. I'll go get Jack." The words raced out of my mouth, fast but quiet. I looked at Nicole and Katie, each putting their full body weight on the door. After a beat, they looked at each other, then back at me.

"You sure?" Katie asked.

"Yeah, otherwise we have nothing," I replied. "We don't want to wait for something bad to happen first."

"Okay." Katie answered. "Be careful."

"I will." I answered. This sounds crazy, but I felt like I could even dodge bullets at that point. I mean, I had full belief in the power of adrenaline to get me to Jack's house faster than anyone. That moment in the pole barn was a chance to exercise my belief, and I knew it.

They pressed their ears to the door to get more clues as to what was happening outside. I wasn't close enough to put my ear at the door, but I listened hard too.

"So what you gonna do, honey?" the voice asked. "You gonna let us in?"

Stephanie answered by firing her rifle.

At that sound, the three of us moved in unison. Katie and Nicole backed up from the door, Nicole grabbing the doorknob to turn it and open it a crack. I grabbed the doorknob, opened the door and sprinted through it toward Jack's house. I hoped they had immediately shut the door behind me, but did not dare turn around to check. And, just like in middle school, my adrenaline kicked in.

I felt nothing but the sensation of flying. The ground wasn't this hard thing made of gravel and earth, it was a springboard for my feet. Any faster and I might have heard the wind whistling past my ears.

Approaching Janet and Jack's house, I wasn't sure if I should start yelling or not, so I didn't. I leapt up their porch stairs in a single bound and yanked open the creaky old screen door. Once inside, I half-yelled, half-wheezed for Janet and Jack to appear.

"What in blazes?" Aunt asked, emerging from the living room.

I breathlessly told her, as quickly as I could, about the people threatening us. Jack immediately sprang into action. He momentarily disappeared, then returned with two rifles. He handed one to me, and one to Janet. He motioned for me to follow him. Janet already seemed to know what to do. As we left the kitchen, I glanced back at her. She checked the gun to make sure it was loaded, and cocked it with the easy assurance of an old pro.

Jack led me through the house and downstairs into the pitch-black cellar. Once there, he whispered "Hold on to me," then led me through the darkness to the other side. As soon as he opened the door, the remaining daylight flooded in to let me see and understand his plan. We crept up the short flight of concrete steps to their backyard.

We circled wide around the house to check it from the front. Nobody was there. I could see Janet in the open kitchen window, watching over their driveway. Jack stopped us at a patch of fragrant lilac trees in the corner of the front yard.

"You wait here," he said. "I'll go see what those assholes are up to."

"You sure?" I asked.

"Yeah. I don't want you or the other girls getting in a situation."

"But you'll be outnumbered."

"That's only if they start a fight, honey. They're on my property, and that counts for a lot out in these parts."

"You want my rifle?" I asked.

"Nah, I keep this with me," he said, lifting his shirt slightly to display a large, black pistol in a military-looking holster. "I'm retired law enforcement. That oughta settle 'em down." He winked at me, then headed towards the pole barn.

I stood there, shielded from view by the lilacs, and started to second guess my perception. Did we blow the situation out of proportion? Stephanie fired a shot, but I hadn't heard one since. Did she just freak out in front of some strangers? Are they gone already? What will Jack find at the pole barn? Good lord, will Stephanie accidentally shoot Jack?

Then I saw movement out of the corner of my eye. One of the men from the van was walking down the middle of the gravel driveway toward the house. I could see a pistol in his hand. My heart stopped. He followed me there?

As he approached the house, I heard Aunt call out.

"You better not take another step, mister," she called out in a very serious voice.

"Well ma'am, I'm just here looking for one of my friends."

"Like hell you are. Now get off my damn property."

He took a step forward, then another.

"That ain't polite, lady."

"I mean it." I looked over at her. She had her rifle pointed right at him, out the kitchen window.

He raised his arms, pistol in his right hand. It looked so fake, like he was trying to prove he was surrendering without meaning it. In just a moment after holding his arms out in surrender, they slowly drifted down closer to his body. I whispered to her not to believe him, and hated him for his deception.

His stance changed suddenly from passive to aggressive. He aimed and fired at Janet.

I couldn't believe what I was seeing. Like in a dream, I raised my rifle and aimed right for his chest, remembering Jack's words. Never point your firearm at anything unless you intend to shoot it. And never shoot something unless you intend to kill it.

But Janet was alive, because she shot back. My relief and hope hit me like a hammer. I lowered my rifle.

I watched him cower momentarily in panic, then raise himself right, aim his weapon again, and fire toward the house.

Then there no sound but the ringing in my ears.

I broke my gaze at him to look at the kitchen window. Janet wasn't there.

Then I knew what I had to do.

I turned my attention back to my rifle and the man at the end of the barrel. He was dead center, standing still, apparently trying to process the fact that he just killed an old lady in her own kitchen for no goddamned reason.

At that moment, I served as judge, jury, and executioner and felt completely okay with it. I pronounced him an asshole who no longer deserved to live. No second guesses.

Inhale, exhale, hold, squeeze.

He dropped to the ground like a ragdoll, his murder weapon clattering to the gravel like a toy.

The ease with which I just shot a fellow human being momentarily blew my mind. To be honest, that numbness lasted for a while after I fired that shot. But there was no time to waste. I had to check on Aunt Janet. I ran past the body in the driveway, up the porch steps, then tried to open the front door. It was locked, of course, but I yanked a couple of times and yelled anyway. Then I remembered the kitchen window, just a few feet away from me.

The window was shattered. A few glass shards crunched under my feet. Janet had removed the screen to point her rifle outward, but the man's first shot must have hit the top half of the window. Holding my breath, I looked in through the shattered glass

Janet laid slumped over on the kitchen floor. Her face was almost unrecognizable for the gunshot wound and the blood flowing from it. The blood was almost black, pooling around her, soaking into her blouse, obliterating its pink floral print inch by inch. Judging by the way the rifle was laying loose beside her, I guessed she was dead before she hit the floor.

Suddenly I remembered that moment with the bully in our snow fort. We let him destroy our home without ever making him answer for his violation.

Now I am an adult with a gun and no fucks left to give, I thought to myself.

(Of course, I realized since then that was a really creepy, awful moment in my life, and hope I never feel that way again.)

Instead of the adrenaline-fueled sprint to flee, I walked home purposefully, rifle at the ready, not caring if they saw me coming or not.

Jack approached me halfway back to the pole barn, Glock in hand. His face was grim.

"I heard shots so I came back."

"Yeah. I got the bastard."

"What happened?"

"Go look," I said numbly, then kept walking.

While all that was happening at the house, my friends were facing their own fight for their lives.

After Stephanie fired a warning shot toward the men standing in front of the van, they retreated to the van, threw the doors open for cover, and drew their weapons. A third man emerged from the back of the van to run after me. One of the men in front fired back at Stephanie, missing her but hitting the barn inches from her head. She startled and fell backward into the hay, crying out. The girls told me later they were terrified she'd been shot.

Twinkie screamed and bent over Stephanie, sure she'd see blood everywhere, but Stephanie was okay. The bullet missed her completely, but in the process of falling over, a shard of hay landed in her eye, causing sharp pain. She squeezed both eyes shut, cursing incoherently. Twinkie tried to comfort Stephanie, but Stephanie knocked her hands aside.

"I'm okay, just take the gun," she growled. Twinkie did so immediately, then took Stephanie's place at the edge of the hayloft window.

"I don't see them!" Twinkie hissed down at our friends.

While Stephanie was down, the two men crouching behind the van doors moved quickly to take advantage of Stephanie's fall. They ran around the corner to the pole barn's side door, beyond Twinkie's line of sight, and tried to open it. Katie and Nicole's blood turned to ice with fear as they heard their doorknob turn. They leaned as hard as they could against the door to keep it from opening. Shelby and Maggie stood a few feet away, unsure of how to help.

Then one of the men body slammed the door. Katie and Nicole recoiled with an "oof," but leaned back against the door just in time for the next strike. Seconds later, another body slam. Katie lost her footing and slid awkwardly onto her knee, crying out in surprise, but did not let go of the door. Shelby leapt forward with outstretched arms to push on the door above Katie. They wondered if they could keep the men from breaking the door down, and if not, what would happen to them?

As Katie tried to stand back up, while Shelby moved slightly to the side to give her enough room, the man body slammed the door a third and final time. The door gave way, taking some of the door frame with it in a spray of splinters. The man stumbled through the doorway, past the girls scattered around it, clearly as surprised as the girls that he succeeded. He regained his balance, stood up, and looked across our pole barn in confusion. I guess he didn't expect the inside of an old, rural pole barn to look like a twinkly ladies' hair salon.

And there was Maggie, waiting for him.

She brandished the folding lawn chair Breanna always sat on to play video games. And she was ready.

As soon as the man's meandering gaze met her eyes, she swung the lawn chair around and clocked him so hard across the side of the head, he fell dumbly over onto Nicole.

Nicole rolled him off of her, then looked up at Maggie. She was still armed and dangerous, though her weapon was now considerably dented.

"Get out of the way," Maggie said quietly. Nicole retreated further into the pole barn.

Maggie beat the man savagely with the lawn chair, over and over again, until the chair was a bloody tangle of aluminum and fabric and her sister's rapist was a bloody tangle of bone and flesh. Shelby and Katie backed away too, choked speechless by the horror.

The second guy who'd been trying to break into the pole barn had a front row view of the carnage. He raised his gun and pointed it into the pole barn, but all he could see was his friend and flashes of metal, all he could hear was growling and whacking and wailing. So he started backing up slowly, gun still pointed toward the open side door.

And that's what I saw at the end of my walk back from the house. One of Maggie's attackers, a friend of the man who just killed Janet, pointing a gun into my home. I didn't know what else was going on at the time, but I was sure he wasn't there to do us any favors. I raised my rifle, aimed, and fired. He sank like a stone and did not move.

The van suddenly jerked to life. One last guy had moved from the back into the driver's seat, had just closed the driver's side door, and was trying to shift it into gear to leave. One last gunshot from the hayloft made the driver slump over into the horn, causing it to blare continuously. I ran over to the van, pushed the guy over to silence the horn, then turned off the engine. I dusted the windshield crumbles off his wrist and checked it for a pulse. There was none.

Once out of the van, I looked up at the hayloft window. Twinkie waved at me with her free hand and Stephanie's rifle.

17
Afterbirth

Have you ever been a part of a genuinely incredible event that was both confusingly surreal and blisteringly real? Where, as the noise fades and the smoke clears, you just look around and wonder how life is supposed to work after that? The kind of event you read about in viral posts, but wonder if was made-up clickbait?

There I was, standing out on a gravel driveway out in the middle of nowhere, surrounded by dead bodies.

I looked back up to the hayloft window for Twinkie, but she was out of sight. Then I saw Katie, Nicole, and Shelby stepping out of the pole barn.

"Is everyone okay?" I asked.

This was their first moment to see all the things outside they'd only been able to hear. They looked around cautiously before anyone answered me.

"Uh, yeah," Shelby answered slowly. "But uh, Maggie…"

"Is she okay?" Worry managed to bubble up through the numbness.

"Well, she's not bleeding, if that's what you're asking," Shelby replied.

"Where is she?" I asked.

"She's inside," said Katie, kneeling over to inspect the body in the driveway. She looked up at me. "Be careful," she said. "It's gross in there."

Slowly, I walked toward the small side door. The door was dangling a bit off-kilter, and the frame near the doorknob was broken.

Once I reached the doorway, I saw the blood on the floor, a surreal, slowly growing pool of black reflecting the Christmas lights in the rafters.

In the middle of it was the awkward heap of a large man on the floor, whose head didn't really look like a head anymore. The contents of my stomach shot up to the edge of my throat. I closed my eyes and swallowed, trying to mentally erase what I'd just seen, and block out the smell of blood overwhelming my nose. Rabbits have so much less blood than a man.

I opened my eyes, ready to look at anything besides the body, and found Maggie, sitting in a folding chair facing her quarry. A tangled mess of what appeared to be another folding chair lay beside her. She looked strangely freckled, still puffy-eyed, but calm.

"I think the cat got out," she said quietly.

"We'll find him again," I replied gently. "Did this guy break in to the barn?"

"Yeah," she answered.

I glanced back at his body, then back to her.

"And you stopped him?" I asked.

"Yeah."

"And was he one of the..."

"Yeah." She answered numbly.

"Well, GOOD." My anger and my voice began to rise uncontrollably, as I stood up. "See, motherfucker? That's what you get for being an ASSHOLE!" I turned, kicked the body in the legs, then walked outside, taking a deep breath of fresh air.

"ASSHOLE!" I yelled out across the driveway.

Leaves rustled and birds chirped in response, like it was just another normal day.

That's when I started to wonder if we were minutes away from being swarmed by police responding to neighbors' reports of multiple gunshots and screams.

I sat down at our fire pit and quietly waited for the authorities to swarm in, lights flashing, sirens blaring, and take me away.

But nothing happened.

Nicole, Katie, and Shelby sat down around the fire pit with me. We waited some more.

Twinkie came out to meet us, and sat down too.

"Stephanie's okay, she got the piece of hay out of her eye."

"Oh, that's what happened to her?" Katie asked.

"Yeah," Twinkie answered with a sigh.

"She'd better wash her eye out really well, it might be germy." Katie said.

"Yeah. And speaking of…" Twinkie replied. "We have that, uh, situation in the pole barn."

"Do we call the police?" Nicole asked.

We looked at each other, at a loss for words.

"I don't particularly want to go to jail," I finally said.

"Yeah, neither do I. Shelby, did you give the 911 dispatcher our address?" Twinkie asked.

"No. I don't even know our address," Shelby answered.

"I don't think you were on long enough for them to trace the call," I suggested.

"They didn't come to help when we asked them," Shelby reminded us.

"At least we're all okay," Twinkie sighed. "I mean, besides Breanna."

I realized then I had to tell Twinkie about her Aunt Janet. But how to do that? I was so tired and numb, I didn't trust myself to do it right.

"Twinkie."

"What?"

I sighed. "One of the guys went to the house."

"What?"

"I uh…" I said, and lowered my head.

"What are you… are they okay?" She stood up in a panic.

I looked around desperate for help with this, even though nobody else knew what I knew. My eyes caught Shelby's. She must have understood, because she stood up and said mildly, "Come on Twinkie, let's go to the house and see if they need any help." Shelby took her by the hand and walked with her toward the house.

I slumped over to nestle my head in my arms for a moment. When I looked up, I saw Katie and Nicole were looking at me for answers.

"One of the guys… killed Aunt Janet."

They gasped.

They asked me how, and I told them how the guy chased after me because I ran to the house for help. That Aunt died valiantly defending her home as Jack ran to our aid. That stopping her killer was the thing that convinced me to pull the trigger, after being unable to shoot an animal for food.

Katie held her hand to her mouth. Nicole reached out to touch her shoulder. I sat there, realizing I wasn't just delivering bad news, but confessing murder, then curled up into a ball, trying to disappear.

Suddenly their arms were around me, their faces close to mine, their whispers caressing my ears and neck.

"You were so brave."

"I was just trying to do the right thing," I murmured.

"You got the guy in the driveway too, didn't you?"

I raised my head to look at them. "He was pointing his gun into the pole barn! I couldn't let him hurt any of you."

They both squeezed me harder.

"Thank you," Katie whispered.

I hugged them back.

After that, I felt better. Such a weight had been lifted off me. What I did was no longer a secret. And the people who knew, loved me harder for it. And they reminded me that I did it to protect the people I loved most in the world, some of whom might not have survived the day.

I felt good enough to remember the two of us still in the pole barn. Breaking the hug, I stood up and looked back at them.

"Come on," I said. "We have a couple of kick-ass chicks to fix up, and a cleanup on aisle 7."

We were really worried about Maggie in the immediate aftermath. She's always been the meek one, the first to apologize, the last to lose her temper. Plus, who's ever had a worse day than the one she just had?

We walked back in and decided to open the big door for more light and air. The flood of daylight overwhelmed the Christmas lights, transforming the space back into a barn. Maggie remained sitting in the same position I'd left her. Stephanie was in the kitchen area, feeling her way around trying to gathering a couple of towels. I watched as Katie approached her. Stephanie's eyes were squinted shut.

"You okay Stephanie?" I asked.

"I got the hay out," she said. "It still hurts to move my eye. Feels better to keep them both shut."

Katie put her arm around her. "Let me take a look at it. We need to wash it out. If it shows any sign of infection, we'll need to take you to the emergency room. Here, I'll lead you to the water pump." As they passed me on the way out, Katie asked me to boil a gallon of water ASAP for a second rinse.

Quickly, I grabbed our big dutch oven out of the kitchen, beat them to the water pump, filled it, then set it on the hotplate. I could hear Stephanie yell a bit as the cold water from the pump hit her eye.

Next, I turned my attention to Maggie. Nicole was crouching next to her, speaking quietly to her. I was glad to notice the puddle of blood hadn't grown any bigger. The guy was pretty big though, too big for four of us to carry. Then I was struck by a dreadful idea.

"Uh, you guys… should we see if Jack wants to call the police, before we start tampering with the evidence?"

Nicole put her hands to her mouth in horror, but Maggie stood up calmly.

"I don't care who does what, or if I get arrested, or whatever," she said resolutely. "This bastard doesn't belong in here." She looked down at the body disdainfully. "I'll go get Jack's wheelbarrow." She stepped around the body and its puddle casually on her way out.

Stunned, I looked at Nicole. She looked back at me, eyes wide, shrugging. Then we looked back down at the mess we had to deal with. It was so gross, I shall spare you the details.

"So, what do we do?" Nicole asked me.

"Maggie has a point," I said. If cops show up, we can't deny what happened. It's not like we're getting rid of all the evidence."

"But they started it. They killed Breanna. They killed Janet. They tried to kill us," she argued hotly.

"Yeah, but we'd sit in jail until they decided we were innocent. If that's what they decide at all. And best case scenario, we wouldn't get formally charged, but the story would be in the papers. And who knows how that would get blown out of proportion. Maybe they'd even call us some weird feminist cult."

"Ugh," Nicole said. "I didn't think about that." Her gaze grazed the scene once more. "Can we… do you think we could get rid of the evidence?"

"All of it?" I said. "The van and four bodies? What about Aunt Janet?"

"I don't know about her," Nicole said. "But this is a big property, right? Big enough to bury four guys and hide a van?"

"It's not our property, though," I reminded her. Her face fell. "Look, I get it. If we can avoid having all our lives ruined by this, let's do that. But it's going to be Jack's decision to make. It's his land, and he has a wife to bury."

"I know..." Nicole sighed. "It's so sad...."

"Yeah. And we might not like his answer. So... start thinking of what you want to do, if he does call the police."

"What do you mean?"

"Nicole, you had absolutely nothing to do with this. You didn't kill anybody."

"I was here. I saw the whole thing. I would be a witness for you."

"It might screw up the rest of your life, getting dragged into this. And maybe there's enough evidence to let us off the hook without your testimony."

"No, Emily," Nicole countered. She looked at me, straight and still. "I love you guys. I'm not going to duck out of here and watch you take the heat." Then she hugged me.

"Hey," Katie called from around the corner. She was leading Stephanie back from the water pump. Steph's hair and face were wet; her eyes were still closed. "We overheard you just now."

"Yeah," Stephanie said. "We're with you, we're not throwing you under the bus."

I smiled. "Okay then. So now we wait and see what Jack says."

"I'll go check on them, see how they're doing," Katie said. "To be honest, the smell in here is getting to me already."

"Okay," I said. "Here, Stephanie, you want to go lay down on Nicole's bed?" I sidled up to her to replace Katie. Katie looked at me gratefully, then scooted out of the barn. Stephanie agreed, so I led her to Nicole's compartment and tucked her in on the inflatable mattress. The one that originally belonged to Breanna, I thought to myself.

"Thanks," Stephanie said. "Sorry I didn't get a chance to bag one. I hear you shot two of them."

"Yes I did," I said.

"Impressive," she replied. "Congratulations. You're now the badass bitch of the house."

I snorted. "Stephanie, you'll always be the badass bitch of the house. And next time we get invaded by marauders, I'll let you kill most of them."

"Oh, that's generous of you. Very kind," she teased me with a smile on her face. She started to open her eyes to look at me, then yelped in pain and shut them again.

"I want a drink so bad," she said. "Something to knock me out."

"You're in luck then," I replied. "Maggie did bring back supplies. Hold on a second." I ran to the kitchen, where I'd plunked down the supplies brought in earlier, before the brutal interruption. Dug out a bottle of rum, poured her a glass, then brought it to her.

"Sit up," I instructed her. "I have the perfect medicine for you."

"What's that?" she asked hopefully. She sat up and stuck out her hand.

"Rum, the drink of one-eyed pirates." I pressed the glass into her palm.

"Perfect then," she said, sniffing the glass contentedly. "Arr, bottoms up!" She said in a rough growl, and took a big swig.

"You're such a dork, Stephanie," I teased.

"You started it," she teased back.

I rejoined Nicole at the front of the barn, to hear the slow rumble of wheels on gravel. Maggie arrived with Jack's heavy-duty wheelbarrow. We approached her impatiently.

"So, did you talk to Jack? What did they say? What's going on?"

"No, I didn't see them. I did see Katie go into the house. But I just grabbed the wheelbarrow. It was propped up on the side of the other barn."

"Okay," I said, somewhat crestfallen. I was so hoping we'd get the all-clear to just get rid of everything. But it didn't seem like a good idea to badger Jack and Twinkie for answers. We had a job to keep us busy anyway: get rid of the body and the blood in our pole barn.

Nicole held the wheelbarrow steady as Maggie and I heaved the body into it. We each gagged a couple of times. Maggie helped Nicole steer the wheelbarrow out of the barn. Once outside, we looked around, trying to figure out where to put the body.

"Maybe we could just bury it?" Nicole said.

"That would make us look extra guilty," I replied. "Let's just put him behind the van for now."

We wheeled him around. I looked into the van and noticed flies were already buzzing around the body inside. Dead bodies in real life are disgusting, by the way. They look nothing like they do on TV.

"Ugh," I said hesitantly. "I hate to say it, ladies, but we'd better wrap these guys up NOW. Buried or called in, we don't want them laying around for long."

"Would plastic tarp work?" Maggie asked. "I keep a big roll of it in my car. She walked over to her SUV trunk, lifted a panel, and revealed a large cylinder of painter's plastic.

"Perfect," I said. We pulled the body out of the van, laid him next to the big guy, then rolled each of them in plastic. Once we realized we had enough for the other two, we wrapped them tight, but left them where they lay.

Shadows stretched long as we finished wrapping the last body. I stood up, stretched, then saw movement out of the corner of my eye. Maggie's cat was watching us from the edge of the trees. There would be no mistaking his orange fur for any other woodland creature.

"Hey… there's Snickers." I pointed him out to Maggie. She sighed and looked at him.

"Kitty…" she said defeatedly. "Please don't die today. I'm too tired to save you."

We had no appetites of course, just a gnawing emptiness sapping our energy. I looked forward to going home, stripping myself of all the dirt, sweat and blood, and feeling normal again. But of course, we'd forgotten the floor of the pole barn, soaked black with the blood of Breanna's killer.

"Do we, ugh, wash the floor?" Nicole asked as we looked at it, her nose scrunched in disgust and concern.

"I don't think we can wash dirt," Maggie replied. "Maybe dig it out?"

"Yeah," I agreed tiredly. "We can backfill it with other dirt from outside."

"We still have the gardening tools," I said. "Let's just get this done, get this out of here."

Nicole agreed and brought us the pitchforks and shovels. We dug out the bloody dirt, carried it out with the wheelbarrow. By the time we were done dumping it, we were too tired to dig up replacement soil, so we trudged home in the last of the daylight. My arms, legs, and back burned with exhaustion.

Shelby and Katie returned just in time to feed us; finally, after removing the gore from our environment, food regained its appeal. Katie cooked us bacon, egg, and cheese muffins on the hotplate, a welcome comfort food. I tried to offer Stephanie a sandwich, but she was passed out on the bed. Thought it best to let her sleep off the eye injury.

While Katie cooked, Shelby filled us in on Twinkie and Jack. They were taking Janet's death hard, of course. Twinkie, she said, was calm but didn't stop crying, while Jack seemed broken, inside and out.

Jack already decided he didn't want police on his property, so he wasn't going to call. Since we took out all the attackers, there was no one to arrest. They'd already been tried, convicted, and sentenced as far as Jack was concerned. He said he wanted to bury Janet in the backyard next to her garden, since that's what she would have wanted anyway, and burn the others to get rid of them. Katie said she talked him out of that, due to the smell and smoke, so he said he didn't care how we got rid of them. I volunteered to bury the men. Nicole and Katie offered to help.

I remember laying in my hammock that night, with a book on my chest that was now too heavy for my sore muscles and hands to hold up. My one big scented candle was admittedly lit not to read by, but to keep bad guys away, just like my nightlight when I was a kid. I'd had enough for one day.

18

Cutting the Cord

Our entire next day was spent undoing the mess caused by the intruders. We dug one big, sloppy pit and buried the men unceremoniously as far away from our camp, and as deeply into the forest, as we could maneuver the wheelbarrow. Well, I say unceremoniously, but technically, we did each give them a piece of our minds before backfilling their communal grave. I won't write down the words. They're not fit to be written, nor spoken again. And I hope I never meet anyone else who deserves them.

After lunch, Shelby returned from Jack's house. They'd stayed with him all night in an impromptu wake for Aunt Janet. She told us Jack was ready to bury her. We were tired from digging, but this was important. We dared not utter a word of complaint.

Twinkie and Jack decided Janet would want to rest in her rose garden. Her back yard's northwestern corner was filled with two dozen different rose bushes, with a primitive cobblestone path down the middle, punctuated by a large pea gravel circle. In the center of the circle, a cement angel with a harp stood on a pedestal. They decided to make the angel and pedestal her headstone.

We moved the pedestal and angel back, dragged the pea gravel out of the way, then carefully dug a deep, tidy grave. It took us all afternoon, because we were already worn out, and we were determined to do a good job. The shadows stretched long across the garden by the time her final resting place was ready.

We ran back to the barn long enough to wash ourselves clean and change into the most respectable clothes we had. I helped Stephanie get ready, because her eye injury caused her to keep her eyes shut for comfort. We walked solemnly back to the house together for the funeral service.

Twinkie had cleaned and dressed Janet in her favorite dress, and wrapped her in a bolt of fresh muslin. Twinkie, Shelby, Maggie and Jack carried her little body to the garden silently. We used ropes to gently lead her down to the bottom of the grave. Then we each picked a rose off a nearby bush and waited for Twinkie and Jack to speak.

Twinkie went first.

"I can't tell you how much I love my aunt Janet. My whole life, she's been so warm and loving to my whole family, even my Dad. I remember, Mom said Janet was scared that her baby sister was dating a Muslim, until he came over and ate two plates of her fried chicken and two slices of her chess pie. She said anybody who loved her cooking that much must be all right." Twinkie half chuckled and sniffed.

"As long as I can remember, Janet always had her home open for company, ready to welcome anyone any time with fresh baked cookies, fresh flowers, and just, love and hugs and smiles. And she taught me the old American ways to keep house. I fell in love with how she did it. I learned everything from her. I will always try to be as good a hostess as her. Goodbye."

There were tears in her eyes, her voice was thick with emotion, but her face was as resolute as always. It was that moment I realized just how much Janet had meant to Twinkie, and even though we'd been best friends forever, I never really noticed. That's when I really started crying.

It was Jack's turn to speak. For a moment, he couldn't. The silence as we watched this weathered old man struggle to find words for his loss choked us all up. It was heavy, so heavy, even though we were surrounded by the light beauty of the garden and the vibrant sunset. Finally, he spoke.

"Janet…. I'm sorry I can't give you a better service. But you never wanted anyone to make a big fuss about you anyway…" He looked down for a moment to compose himself. "You was a good woman, and you always did right by your family. I just wish I could've…." Jack stopped there, overcome by grief. We tossed our roses onto Janet, then surrounded him and led him back to his house.

Twinkie and Shelby stayed in the house with Jack. Maggie, Nicole, Katie, Stephanie and I said our goodbyes, then we diggers worked together to fill Janet's grave in silence. Our nice funeral clothes got dirty but that seemed fitting to me, because I had a part in her death. I couldn't shake the thought that everything I'd set into motion led me to this moment – standing there in the waning daylight, shovel in my hands, laying to rest a life that shouldn't have ended, a soul that needed to be on Earth.

Finally, we finished burying Janet and walked home together, Stephanie holding my arm to guide her back down the path.

Stephanie was the one to break the silence. She leaned closer to my head and spoke quietly.

"You seem upset."

"Yeah, I just attended a funeral," I answered brusquely.

"Duh. There's no need to be flip about it. Like, you aren't just sad, you're unsettled."

"You can feel that through my arm, huh?"

"Now I know you feel unsettled. You're acting like a shithead."

I sighed.

"I just… I keep thinking, if I hadn't run for help –"

"Okay, stop right there," Nicole cut in. "We needed help. What would have happened to us if you hadn't gone back for your gun?"

"But I led him right to her!" I cried.

"Come on," Stephanie reasoned. "The driveway led him to her. Even if they'd killed us all at the barn, they probably wouldn't have stopped there."

"I should have shot him sooner," I argued.

"Sweetie, I know you," Stephanie said soothingly. "You wouldn't have been able to pull the trigger before you did. You have a strong conscience, and you followed it every step of the way."

Katie put her arm over my shoulder, on the other side of Stephanie.

"You know what this is, right?"

I looked at her and sighed.

"Bargaining?"

"Yeah. Bargaining."

"I know. I read about stages of grief. I just never felt them so hard before."

It was true. I felt yanked. Like, the world was off-balance and I caused it.

Then I remembered what Maggie was dealing with, and felt ashamed to have voiced my little sliver of grief. She lost her sister yesterday. And she saw it. And it wasn't fair. I turned to watch her calmly walking home like it was just another day. I tipped my head to Katie to direct her attention to Maggie. Katie inhaled delicately, as if she might break her next words.

"Maggie?" Katie said gently. "How are you holding up?"

"I'm still numb," Maggie said blandly. "I keep thinking she might come back, even though I know she won't."

"Yeah," Nicole said sadly.

"I'm not sorry I killed the guy that did it though," she said with a suddenly stronger voice. "I never did that before, you know, took an eye for an eye. I always just turned the other cheek."

"Does that make it easier to live with?" I asked.

"It does now," she replied. "I hope it still does later."

Shelby came home at dusk, but Twinkie stayed with Jack at the house. Shelby said they didn't think Jack was ready to be alone yet. The next day, we mostly laid in our hammocks, sleeping or reading, finally unwinding in the first peace and quiet we'd had in days. Nicole spent hours cuddling with Maggie.

I never give Nicole enough credit for being a warm, nurturing person. Her currency is touch and energy. Twinkie's currency of affection, on the other hand, is cocktails and hors d'oevres, infinitely more comfortable to an introvert like me. I'm glad Nicole's available for Maggie, an introvert who nevertheless sometimes painfully craves affection.

Twinkie returned the next morning somewhat disheveled. I watched her walk up the path while I was building the morning fire.

"You okay?" I asked her as she approached.

"Yeah, I'm just tired," she explained. "I didn't plan on staying there overnight, but I should have realized I would need to. He's pretty broken up."

"I'm so sorry, Twinkie," I answered.

"It's okay," she said, looking at me with as much assurance as she could probably muster. "I think he's getting a handle on it. He finally got a decent night's sleep last night. He even cooked me breakfast this morning. Sausage and eggs."

"Well that's a good sign," I commented. "Oh, wait, that's—"

"Haram, I know," Twinkie said, "but I wasn't about to turn it down. So I snuck it to the dog under the table."

"Wait, did I just hear the Muslim chick's handing out sausage, and didn't bring us any?" Stephanie joked. She'd stepped outside on her own, both eyes open for the first time in two days.

"Your eye's all better?" I asked.

"Oh yeah, feels fine now," Stephanie responded. "Eyes don't take long to heal."

"I'm relieved," I told her. "I was envisioning a future with your blind ass hanging onto my arm, telling me I'm going the wrong direction, for the rest of my life."

Stephanie chuckled. "Yeah, but you're the one with direction sense. You'd know I was just saying it to fuck with you."

"Exactly. Well, I bet you're both still hungry. Let me cook you some breakfast." I poked the fire with a steady hand, so glad my friends were feeling better.

"That would be lovely," Twinkie said with a tired smile.

That night, we rested around the campfire, the first night in forever that felt almost normal.

"Anybody want some bourbon?" Stephanie asked. "Sure, we all do."

She pulled a bottle from Maggie and Breanna's trip to town and passed it around. It was the first time we'd all had a drink since the attack. Pretty soon, most of us were gabbing loudly. Suddenly, in a lull, Twinkie broke her silence.

"Do you remember why we all came out here?"

We sat silently, hoping that was a rhetorical question she was about to answer.

"Freedom. We're out here to be free of bullshit and hate. I thought it was gonna be easier. I thought I could make it awesome. I'm sorry I failed."

"You didn't fail!' Nicole said.

"No. It's been a mess. Look what we deal with on a daily basis."

"You never promised us life was going to be easy," Stephanie asked. "I mean, come on."

We chewed on that for a moment in silence.

"Nobody told us life was easy – and if they did, they were asshats and liars… or helicopter parents," Steph continued. "We chose to trade one kind of hardship for another when we came out here. This life out here isn't as ugly or hard as watching people get beaten, harassed, arrested, or killed by the people we pay to protect us, and trying to ignore it, trying to anesthetize ourselves with cute cat videos and pumpkin spice lattes like shit ain't happening. That isn't freedom. Choosing what your world is made of, regardless of the hardship attached to it, that's freedom. And that's what we have, blood and tears and dirt be damned. We are nasty. Let's be proud of it."

19

Mothering

Thankfully, time passed uneventfully for a while. Wounds healed. Grief slowly gave way to acceptance. Twinkie and Maggie seemed to become even closer after sharing such tragic losses. They spent a lot of time out in the woods together, walking and talking. The rest of us tried to make life as easy for them as we could.

Meanwhile, we endeavored to repair all the collateral damage suffered during the attack. Katie fixed the door frame to our barn. Nicole camouflaged the attackers' grave with dead brush. I finished backfilling the pit we dug out of the floor to relieve ourselves of the stain of Breanna's rapist.

We finally remembered to empty Maggie's SUV of their shopping goods. The bacon was a lost cause after slow-roasting in the car for days, but the rest of it was fine. Maggie and Breanna bought hardware and materials for Katie, more seeds, plus spices and ingredients to help us prepare fresh venison, rabbit and chicken.

We realized we could never use the attackers' van for transportation and were afraid to get caught ditching it. So we decided to scrap it and bury any parts we couldn't use. Nicole had the crazy idea of converting it to a greenhouse for the winter. We spent a couple of weeks off and on cleaning it, gutting it, and moving it to an optimal location, a sunny clearing not far from the barn. Nicole started testing its greenhouse capabilities with the seeds of our least favorite vegetables.

Steph spent a lot more time hunting without me. The first couple of times she went out, she tried asking Jack if he wanted to join her, but he was always either drunk or sleeping. I suspect at least one of those "hunting trips" was actually Stephanie and Jack hanging out in the woods with a bottle of whiskey, but I didn't say anything. She's entitled to do what she wants, especially since we're not hurting for food. Besides, she did usually return clear-headed with rabbits, so who knows. Knowing Stephanie was meeting regularly with Jack took some of the pressure off of Twinkie to watch over her uncle. It's hard feeling like you're the only person available to take care of another person, especially their emotional needs.

And Snickers… Contrary to Maggie's worst fears, her cat had taken quite readily to outdoor living. He seemed happier, livelier, and leaner. Snickers came to say hello sometimes when we were outside near the barn. He'd trot up, meow a bit, rub our legs and purr. He'd let Maggie pick him up, but would struggle when she tried to carry him back inside. So she quit trying. After a couple of weeks of freedom, he finally tried to re-enter the barn. That was a mistake letting him in! After that, he demonstrated the quintessential feline habit of wanting to be in the barn when we shut him out, and wanting to be outside when we shut him in. But he was a happy cat, so she wasn't worried about him anymore. We set out fresh water for him, but no longer food, as he seemed to have adapted to a wildlife diet. We thought it wise not to ask questions.

It took a couple of weeks for Maggie and Twinkie to emerge from their shroud of grief and rejoin our life together. Thankfully it wasn't too difficult for the rest of us to fill in for them while they processed their losses. I took a fresh accounting of our food stash, storage, and finances, prepared estimates, and discussed them with the other girls. We'd be doing okay for several more months, thanks to Maggie and Breanna's last trip, our poultry, and Stephanie's ongoing hunt.

Breanna's chickens were still growing strong, well on their way to maturity. I did most of the caretaking, since I had spent time trying to learn from Breanna how to raise them, all the while taking notes. Reading the notes helped a lot, but for a while made me sad every time I read them. Breanna was all right, you know… she just needed something to belong to.

It was kind of funny though, about a month after Breanna died, I was doing my daily chick chores. Suddenly I realized we had male chickens and female chickens and I wasn't sure which was which – and that would be pretty important to find out, otherwise we'd end up with a mountain of chickens and no eggs to eat. A boatload of chickens. Whatever the technical term is for way too many chickens.

So I peered more closely at them while they chowed down on their chickie breakfast. They didn't seem terribly different from each other. No one chicken seemed bigger than the other. They weren't different colors. And obviously, none of them were sporting visible genitalia. Generally, I prefer animals that way, but I had business to attend to.

I picked one up, flipped it forward, and started examining its little feathered chicken bottom. Just then, Shelby walked up behind me.

"Whatcha doing?" she asked.

"Trying to sex this chicken," I answered.

"What?" she asked, alarmed. She looked down at the chick in my hand, then started backing up. "Why?!" She exclaimed, half horrified, half laughing. "That's so wrong!"

Maggie and Nicole, tending the garden nearby, came over to see what the ruckus was about.

"What's so wrong?" Nicole asked.

"Emily has to masturbate the chickens," Shelby cried, her face contorted with exaggerated disgust.

"WHAT?" Maggie and Nicole said, wrinkling their noses.

"No! Sexing them, identifying the males from the females," I explained.

"You have to masturbate them to see who is who?" Nicole asked, aghast.

"No, "sexing" is just the word for identification. I do NOT have to masturbate the chickens."

"Oh thank god," Maggie cried in relief.

"Yeah," Shelby said. "I was afraid you were going to ask me for help."

"That's funny, because I actually was gonna ask you to help," I replied, "so I'm glad we cleared up that little confusion. I have to identify the males from the females so we can separate them."

"Ah, I see." She looked at my chicken, then looked down at our little flock. "You're holding a male."

"Seriously?" I looked down at the chick in my hands.

"Yeah…" She looked at me like that was an absurd question.

"Don't ask her how she knows," Maggie replied, one eyebrow raised. "That's probably TMI."

"Maggie, what exactly are you implying?" Shelby said pointedly.

"I'm just teasing."

"Well anyway," Shelby turned from her to me and my chick, "here, let me show you." She took my chick and pointed at his head. "See this thing running down between his eyes? It sticks out more on his head than, say, that chick." She walked over to pick up another chick. "See? Hers barely sticks up at all."

"Ah," I said with a sigh of relief. "Yay, I don't have to inspect chicken butts anymore!"

"Yeah, that is easy," Maggie agreed. "Shelby, how did you know that?"

"Most guys are the same," she answered. "They gotta have something to show off."

20

Reality Encroacheth

Jack Miller, had a simple life and simple desires. Born and raised in that old country house, he bought it from his parents with 20 years of savings from his factory wages so they could afford to retire. Janet and Jack later moved in to help his parents conclude their lives quietly in their own home, die in their own bed. After they passed away, he inherited the property and stayed so Janet could live the homesteader life she'd always wanted.

Jack was always proud of the endless work he did to care for his parents and his wife. Work at the factory, come home, work on the homestead, go to bed, start again the next morning. He was never terribly interested in the rest of the world. What did it offer but more reasons to work, more needs to remain perpetually unmet?

Once his folks and wife were gone, the house was just an empty shell, one he couldn't possibly fill by himself. Stephanie said he once broached the possibility of inviting the women to move into the house with him. But he said, "Fish and visitors stink after three days," and she couldn't disagree. He said he liked his peace and quiet.

About three weeks after we buried Janet, Stephanie found Jack slumped over at the base of a tree near a clearing behind the house, with a bone-dry bottle hanging off his lap, and his dog laying at his feet like he did every evening at home. The dog immediately greeted Steph with a bark and a whine. He didn't immediately want to follow her back, but she coaxed him back to the house and shut him in.

She came back and told me first. Pulled me away from the clothesline and dragged me into the forest several yards.

"What the what?" I asked.

Stephanie told me what she found.

"Oh no…." I sighed and shook my head.

"Yeah. Help me tell Twinkie?"

We were silent for a moment.

"Did he leave a note?"

"No, but it's not like it's a mystery." She shrugged.

"You saw this coming? I don't think she did. She was finally relaxing about him."

"Yeah, I saw it coming. But I didn't want to bother her with it. It's not her business."

"Yeah, it kind of is her business. He's family," I argued.

"Twinkie couldn't have stopped him. She would have only made him feel guilty about it," she replied.

"You don't think knowing she cares would have stopped him?" I asked.

"He knew she cared, but he also knew she had her own life," Stephanie explained. "I think he just decided his own life was over, and he didn't want to start a new one."

"Were you guys talking about it, when you were over there?" I asked.

"Not really. I don't get into other people's business, and he wasn't much of a talker. So no, he wasn't talking about killing himself, and I wasn't trying to talk him into it."

"Not suggesting you were," I said defensively.

"I'm just saying I understand. And I'm asking you to help me break it to Twinkie without her freaking out about it."

"Okay," I said, looking into her eyes. Her face softened.

"Thanks."

Twinkie took it well as could be expected. She cried off and on over the next several days. Steph and I buried him next to the tree where we found him, quietly, without ceremony, the way we guessed he would have wanted it.

That left us with an empty house, a second coop with a half dozen adult hens, and the dog. Even though the house was a lot more comfortable, none of us wanted to move into it. Twinkie called to transfer the utilities to her name. We didn't want to lose our electricity, but we couldn't afford to pay for the second house, so we shut off everything in the house but the fridge and chest freezer. The second coop was suddenly really handy, now that we knew we'd need a rooster coop and a hen coop. Maggie, naturally, took the dog, an Australian shepherd. He was a good boy. He seemed uneasy staying in the barn with us, but perked up whenever he was outside, back in more familiar territory.

Our world, on the other hand, seemed to be shrinking and shrinking. We were more comfortable with our primitive lifestyle than before, but I wondered if it was because we were just avoiding everything else - Jack's house, town, the news, such as it was... nothing but third-rate, nauseating nationalist propaganda. It was weird too, after living so far removed from pop culture, its news seemed dull and predictable.

Foremost in our minds, however, was always the fear that someone would approach us about the van, the missing assholes, or Twinkie's folks. The likelihood that anyone would ask us questions was slim, but in our heads, it was huge. Murphy's Law can be a real bitch.

One day, while we were all doing our daily chores, Stephanie stuck her foot with a dirty knife.

"Wow! Holy shit fuck!" I heard her yell.

I trotted around the corner to see her looking down at her worn old canvas shoe with a 10 inch knife poking straight up out of it.

"Ew," I grimaced.

"Uck…" she said, grimacing too. She pulled the knife out, then pushed off her shoe. Her sock was already soaked in blood.

"Oh shit," she said, then passed out.

I raced over to her and called for help. The others all ran over to encircle us.

"What happened?" Katie asked worriedly.

"Oh my god, is she dead?!" Maggie cried.

"No, I think she just passed out," I said. I crawled around to her head and picked it up to rest it on the side of my shin.

"Maybe she's dead! That's a lot of blood!" Maggie cried.

"It's not that much blood," Katie said reassuringly.

As if in response, Stephanie stirred.

"I'm gonna puke…" she said. "My blood freaks me out."

"You're gonna be okay," I said.

"Look," Katie said. She peeled the bloody sock off Stephanie's foot. "Look, it's not even bleeding much anymore."

"I still don't want to look at it," Stephanie replied gruffly, turning her face away.

"You don't have to, we'll clean it up," I soothed her. "Do you still feel like throwing up?"

"Just don't let me look at it, I'll be okay in a minute." she replied.

"How do you handle your period?" Shelby asked.

"It's not the same. It's not an injury," Stephanie answered. "I don't like seeing my body injured."

"Look," Nicole said, holding out the knife with two fingers like a dirty gym sock. "This knife is gross. What were you doing with it?"

"Skinning rabbits," Stephanie answered.

"Steph, that's my job, I told you I'd do that," I chided her.

"Yeah, but you hung up my laundry today, so I wanted to return the favor."

"You guys, we're gonna need to clean that wound, and she might need some antibiotics," Nicole said grimly. "That thing is nasty." She set the knife down in disgust.

"I'll go get some hot water and clean towels," Katie offered.

While Katie was fixing up Stephanie, the rest of us stepped aside to devise a plan.

"We're gonna need to go to town," Maggie said. "I don't want to though."

"I'm not going anywhere!" Stephanie yelled. "I'm staying right here. With an emphasis on not walking."

"We're not asking you to!" I yelled back in response.

"Okay!" Stephanie answered.

"I'll go," I offered. "But I don't know how to get antibiotics."

Shelby chimed in. "I might be able to hook us up. I know a pharmacist up northwest. He wouldn't sell us any hard stuff, but he should be able to sell us antibiotics without a prescription no problem."

"That'll work," I said. "Come with me?"

"Yeah, sure," Shelby nodded.

"Hey Nicole, come help me pick her up," Katie called. Nicole trotted off. Shelby and Twinkie wandered back as well.

"Maggie, can I talk to you for a second?"

"Sure, what's up?"

"I think you should come out with us."

"Why?"

"Do you not want to go because you're afraid?"

"Well, yeah."

"That's the reason why you should go. You can't be afraid to go back into town forever. And the longer you wait, the harder it might be."

Maggie sighed.

"You don't want to end up a shut-in, do you?" I countered. "Never see your house again?"

She sighed again.

"Maybe I don't want my house anymore."

"Come on…." I said, hugging her. "We'll go together. We'll go to your house to check on it, we'll go to the pharmacy, you can get some magazines or something. Death by chocolate ice cream."

"I haven't had ice cream in forever. Since you know…."

"We'll get you some ice cream, then come back. Everything will be okay. I promise. Trust me."

She looked at me hard for a moment, then nodded.

Shelby called her pharmacist friend, Charlie, who confirmed an under-the-table sale of a bottle of antibiotics. Twinkie and I walked over to Jack's house to borrow a pistol from his hidden stash. She didn't like the idea of my carrying, but I didn't like the idea of going unarmed. I knew I promised Maggie everything would be okay. Inside, though, I felt like I couldn't promise that unless I knew we had something to defend ourselves. I was trying to be brave, but yeah, I was scared too. I was forcing myself to go too, just like I talked Maggie into it, and for the same reason. I needed to stop being scared.

21

A Rose in the Thorns

Shelby drove us to town in her car. It felt shockingly sleek and comfortable after months of hammocks, logs, and lawn chairs.

"Wow, I feel like I could fall asleep back here," I said, stretching my legs out across the backseat.

"Yeah," Maggie said from the front. "So plush."

"You guys have been gone for too long," Shelby laughed.

"Can we stop by the library?" I asked.

"There's one near my house," Maggie answered. "When we get there, I'll show you."

We stopped at the pharmacy first, and all went in. It was my first immersion in the outside world in months. Everything seemed so bright and loud and jarring… and irrelevant.

"Wow," I whispered to myself.

Maggie and I followed Shelby to the pharmacist's counter, and hung back together as she spoke to him. Neither one of us wanted to stray too far from the others. We watched Shelby smile and talk with her friend. She came back with a bag and a puzzled look on her face.

"Everything okay?" Maggie asked.

"Yeah, I guess… I got the antibiotics," Shelby replied. We browsed the goodies aisles for a minute and bought a few treats for the gang. I can't lie, I started salivating when I saw the chocolates. I picked out a little bag of dark chocolate covered caramels for myself, sour gummies for Katie, wasabi almonds for Nicole, and chocolate-covered blueberries for Twinkie. (Did you think I'd get her Twinkies? Nope… eating hundreds of them in elementary school was all she could stand.)

Once back in the car, Shelby abruptly said, "That was weird."

"What?"

"Remember I told you Charlie doesn't sell recreational drugs on the DL?"

"Yeah."

"He just tried to hook me up with a bottle of opioids."

"Did you buy it?" I asked.

"No way. The last thing we need is Stephanie on Opes."

"That's what I was thinking too," I agreed. Steph's already an alcoholic, and Opes are monsters.

"Do you think he was trying to set you up?" Maggie asked worriedly.

"I don't know," Shelby answered. "Maybe he thought the antibiotics were just an excuse or a ruse or something."

"You'd think they'd be trying to discourage people from using Opes," Maggie said. "It destroys people."

"Let me have the bag," I said suddenly. Maggie handed it back to me. Only one bottle inside. I opened it to see big chalky tablets.

"Well, he gave us what we asked for," I confirmed. "But you know what they say about antibiotics, they're a gateway drug for the hard stuff."

"Like what, laxatives?" Shelby asked.

"Yeah. We'll be freebasing suppositories before you know it," I continued. "We'll be shoving them up each other's noses for kicks!"

"Oh, you guys are terrible!" Maggie laughed.

Next, we drove to Maggie's neighborhood, an older middle-class suburb full of modest 1980's ranches. It seemed quiet and peaceful, but after a moment I noticed little differences from how it used to be. More doors and windows had incongruous iron bars guarding them. Curtains blacked out every window. No toys littering a lawn, no flowers in beds or boxes. More grass looked overgrown. It looked like half of Maggie's neighborhood was now prepared for some sort of siege. On several of the doors I saw a small white sticker with a black triangle on it. Like a flag, but I didn't recognize it.

We parked at Maggie's house; we were the only activity on the quiet street. Maggie pointed out the direction of the library, just a few blocks from her house, at the end of the street. It was so close, and it felt so novel to be out, I decided to walk there.

"Are you sure?" Maggie asked.

"Yeah, I'm sure. I won't be long." I patted my purse to remind her I wasn't completely defenseless, and waved goodbye with a smile.

I walked purposefully down the winding, curvy suburban street to its end, then scanned the buildings across the street. From there, I spied a modest brick church on the left and the library next to it on the right.

I crossed the street, gazing at the church along the way. Its weekly message sign was blank. There were no cars in its parking lot, nor were there any cars at the library. They both looked closed. As I reached the sidewalk, I noticed a single LED candle in the church's front window. It was the only window nearby that wasn't boarded up or blacked out.

I kept thinking about that candle as I approached the library. The library doors were locked. I peered into the window, hoping for some sign of life, but there was none, not even an illuminated emergency exit light. I stepped back to examine the building – the grass was overgrown. Had anyone been here in the last few months? I wistfully grabbed the handle and rattled it, hoping it was just stuck.

Disappointed and confused, I headed back across the library parking lot and past the church next door to it. Then I paused in front of the church steps, thoughtful. Why is the light on? Is anyone home? I climbed the steps and tried the door. It was unlocked. But does anyone ever lock a church?

I have to admit, I'm not a very spiritual person, and certainly not religious. I went with my friends a few times; read bits and pieces of the Old and New Testaments. But I was honestly surprised it was still open, still dimly lit, like it hadn't been affected by all the other chaos going on around it.

Standing in the center aisle, looking around at the carved wood pews and simple stained glass windows, I felt an urge to sing something pretty. I didn't know any hymns. Tried remembering the Lord's Prayer song I heard at weddings but couldn't remember the melody. But I did know lots of Christmas songs, so I started to sing one of my favorites.

> *Oh come, all ye faithful, joyful and triumphant,*
> *Oh come, ye oh come ye to Bethlehem.*
> *Come, and behold him,*
> *Born the king of Israel,*
> *Oh come--*

Suddenly I heard a door creak open. My voice faltered. I turned toward the sound and saw a black woman about my mom's age appear from the side, apparently just as surprised to see me as I was to see her.

"Hello?" I said. "I'm sorry, please excuse me."

"For what, the singing?" she asked incredulously.

"Yeah, it was an accident, really."

"Why were you singing it?" She looked suspicious.

"I don't know, it seems kind of silly, right? Singing Christmas songs in September…."

Suddenly an older black lady in a pink Sunday dress appeared behind her. "Oh good, my yarn is here—"

"Shh, mama," the woman snapped at her.

"Who are you?" the old lady asked me just as suspiciously.

I backed up a step. "I'm sorry, I just stopped by on my way to the library, and started singing. I don't mean to disturb you."

"Mama, she wasn't sent here," the woman murmured to her mother.

"Oh, yes she was, I heard it! The Good Lord sent her!" The old lady scooted past her daughter and grabbed me by the hands. "Come on in, honey, let us get a look at you."

"Mama!" the woman pleaded, then looked at me. I stared bewildered back at her. I had no idea what was going on. But I let the old woman lead me through the side door into a Sunday school room. In one corner of the room was a hatch in the floor. A rug had been affixed to the hatch to cover it when the hatch was closed. She gestured me to take the stairs revealed by the open hatch.

"Mama!" The woman cried. "We don't even know this woman!"

"The Lord sent her! Why else would she just wander in here and give the signal?"

The woman behind us sighed, exasperated.

I paused, unsure what to do. The old lady took me by the hand and led me downstairs to a room that reminded me a lot of our pole barn. Strings of Christmas lights illuminated a room full of vintage velvet-upholstered wingback chairs, a couple of school desks and chairs, beanbags and cots. Floral quilts hung from the ceiling to divide the room here and there, just like our home. The walls were peppered with mass-produced depictions of Jesus. About a dozen Hispanic people in casual clusters looked up, clearly shocked to see me. I didn't know what to say or do. Neither did they.

"You wouldn't believe what just happened! The Lord sent us this woman! What's your name, honey?"

"Emily," I answered meekly. "Um, I don't really understand what's going on…."

The first woman, standing behind me, spoke.

"We've all been staying here in hiding. It's not safe for us out there these days, you know. We have some friends who help us sometimes. They let us know they're here by singing the song you were singing."

"Whoa," I breathed. Now the old lady's reaction made sense.

"And we were expecting a visitor today. We just didn't expect you. And you said nobody sent you."

"Right. I had no idea any of this was here."

"And we would like to keep it that way," piped up the man who had been sitting in the corner with a little girl, presumably his daughter. "Abuela, I think we should just ask her to leave now."

"We're in hiding too..." I said suddenly. "We started camping out in the woods months ago. Some of my friends would have had a hard time if we hadn't." I swallowed hard. "So I don't know if that's the same thing you're talking about, but I think I understand."

"But you're white," the old lady said.

"Not all of us," I replied. "But we take care of each other."

"Because that's what Jesus wants us to do, take care of each other," the old lady said, coming closer to shake my hand. "My name is Rose."

"Miss Rose, it's nice to meet you. Nice to meet all of you," I offered awkwardly, looking around at the little group. My social anxiety was kicking in big time, this being such an awkward situation – but I was determined not to screw it up.

"Look, I was just checking out the library to see if it was open," I explained. "A couple of my camp mates are waiting for me down the street, and might get worried if I'm gone too long. So I should be going… Or, um, would you like to meet them?" I asked hesitantly.

The adults glanced at each other. Rose, meanwhile, was still holding my hand. Hers was paper thin skin over knobby bones; soft, cool, and delicate. I looked down at her (she was barely five feet tall) from her hands to her face. She was still smiling warmly up at me.

"I think that's exactly what we should do," Rose announced to her group. "This may be the answer to some of our prayers."

I looked nervously at her daughter, who was watching us both.

"I don't know what we could…" I stammered, "I mean, we can help you if you need it…"

"It's okay, you don't have to understand the plan," Rose said. "Jesus knows the plan." She let go of my hand and started walking back up the stairs, slowly.

Rose's daughter approached me. I turned to her and whispered.

"I'm sorry, I don't know what to do. I don't want to upset her…"

Rose's daughter gave me a little smile.

"You're giving her hope, and that's what she's been praying for. I don't think you're out to harm us. My name is Grace." She offered her hand. I shook it and smiled.

"Oh gosh no. We're on your side! And to be honest, I'm glad I found you. I was beginning to wonder if we were the only people who thought the world had gone sour."

"Don't get me wrong," she said grimly. "It's dangerous out there for us. Not so much for you. You can pass through. We could get picked up on sight."

"Jesus, that's…" I said, then clapped my hand to my mouth. "Excuse me."

A little boy walked up to me from the corner. He eyed me for a moment and said, "Do you like Jesus?"

I looked down to him, smiled and said, "I like all the good guys, and Jesus too." I hoped that was good enough for him.

I turned back to Grace. "Hold on, let me get my friends."

"Please…" Grace implored. "Don't give us away." She stared at me. I nodded to her.

"I will be careful," I assured her. I walked back upstairs, promised Rose I would be right back, checked the window for passersby, then walked briskly across the street and back to Maggie's house. Maggie and Shelby were just locking up.

"Hey, let's go back inside for a minute…" I said. "I have news."

22

Tapping Courage

I told Shelby and Maggie everything. They were both as surprised as I was.

"I think they just want to meet some friendly faces," I explained. "It's a decent-sized building, but they're even more cooped up than we are."

"How many people were in there?" Shelby asked.

"I'd guess two families and the two black ladies, so, maybe 15 people?"

"Wow. And you said they were waiting for someone?"

"Yeah, but they didn't explain, and I didn't want to seem nosy. Most of them didn't seem to trust me, which is understandable."

"Maybe they have a network. Like an underground railroad," Maggie surmised.

"Maybe," I replied. "And that might be a good thing for us. We're pretty isolated."

"And maybe we're a good thing for them," Shelby said. "Like Grace said, we can travel in places they can't. We might be able to help them with supplies in an emergency."

"Yeah, and I would like to do that," I said. Maggie shook her head hard in agreement.

"It's settled then," Shelby said, standing up. "Let's go introduce ourselves."

The introduction went well. Shelby passed the candy we'd bought from the pharmacy to the kids. We offered Grace the antibiotics too, but she politely refused them. We spent a few minutes telling Rose and Grace our own path to living off the grid.

"Our congregation has always been about community," Rose explained in a slow, measured cadence after offering us a cup of coffee. "So one of the things we offered was a Spanish language service every Sunday, and a Sunday school in both Spanish and English for the kids." She looked over at a couple of the kids, reading in their beanbags, and smiled at them.

"Mama ran a day care center too, upstairs," Grace added.

"That's right. We were close to our Hispanic brothers and sisters in our community. We tried to make them feel welcome. So when we started noticing fewer and fewer people attending our service, we talked to them to find out why."

Grace nodded.

"And they said they were afraid to stay here, what with the harassment and violence reported all over the country. The police are splitting families apart, arresting and jailing mothers and fathers, and taking the kids Lord knows where. And the police turn a blind eye when wayward people harass and attack them on the street." Rose shook her head and tsked.

"So Mama decided she had to do something," Grace chimed in. "She went to each remaining family in the Hispanic congregation and quietly offered to let them stay at the church if they ever felt unsafe in their neighborhoods. About a week later, these two families," (she waved her hand toward the others) "called Mama and asked if they could stay. We snuck them in, in the middle of the night. They've been here ever since."

"I think more would have come if I had asked Donna to interpret," Rose said sadly. Grace patted her on the shoulder.

"Mama, you did your best."

"My Spanish is really not that good. For all I know, I might have accidentally been telling them *not* to come back."

"Mama, you worry too much."

"These folks knew enough English that I could talk to them regular," Rose explained. "They accepted our invitation."

"And for a couple of weeks, Mama was their lifeline," Grace added.

"I came to visit them every day. I brought them home cooked food, videos for the kids so they could keep learning." A Hispanic woman sat down with us. She looked tired but clear-eyed, seemingly at peace with the horrible situation she was in. Suddenly it struck me how hard it must be to have children through all this.

"Abuela was an angel," she said. "We always wanted to be able to repay her for her kindness."

"And they got their chance," Rose said matter-of-factly, "because just two weeks later, the police raided *our* neighborhood."

Both Grace and Rose stopped to shake their heads and hum their dissent.

"Oh no," Maggie said. "The one south of downtown?"

Grace nodded. "That's right."

"That's where Katie lived," Maggie said. "She lives with us now."

"I was all alone in our apartment when it happened," Rose explained. "I saw the lights outside through the curtains right before I heard the commotion. Looked out the window and saw a couple of big tanks and trucks and police cars filling up the street. Well, I ain't a dummy, so I grabbed my purse and snuck out the back way and walked all the way to the church. My feet were awful sore by the time I got there."

"Did you two live together?" Maggie asked.

"Yes, Mama lived with me and my husband, Victor," Grace replied. "I work the night shift at the hospital downtown, and my husband works third shift at the penitentiary. I came home the next morning to find police tape and cars blocking off the whole street. I was afraid to ask anybody what was going on. I didn't get close enough to try. I never been so scared, worrying about what happened to Mama. She doesn't carry a cell phone, so I couldn't call her to find out. But I found her here, and called Vic to let him know we were all right."

"He should be back soon," Rose said. "He's out running errands. He's the only one we let go out."

"Why is that?" I asked.

We heard the hatch open and turned to look. Dark pants and thick black shoes descended the staircase, belonging to a very large, very muscled, uniformed black man. His silver badge reflected the light from the open hatch before he closed it. He greeted everyone as he climbed down, then walked over to Grace to kiss her hello. I could see his pistol holstered at his side. He looked very intimidating, which in our situation was a substantial comfort. I figured he looked daunting and official enough to avoid trouble.

"Darlin, I want you to meet our new friends," Grace said. We could finally see Victor had warm, friendly eyes, a velvety baritone voice, and a handshake like a hug. After exchanging greetings, Victor handed Rose a plastic bag. She cooed and pulled out a skein of sunshine yellow yarn. Grace turned back to us to continue their story.

"So after I drove to the church and found Mama, I went back to try to figure out what was going on, you know, try to get back in our apartment. What I didn't understand was, where did everybody go? There was probably at least 100 people living in our building, but I didn't see one of them. They were just gone. And by early afternoon, bulldozers were out there tearing down our building," Grace said sadly. "We couldn't even get our stuff out. All we had left was the clothes on our backs."

"And the church," Rose reminded her.

"And our jobs," Victor added. "We're still going to work like nothing happened. We're the only ones here who can."

"But we still don't know what happened to our neighbors," Grace said worriedly. Victor glanced at her, then at Rose. I suddenly wondered if he knew something.

"That was some operation they had going over there," Victor said. "Based on what Mama told us, it sounds like they were using some hardcore military tactical equipment to raid the neighborhood."

We all fell silent for a moment. Eventually, Rose stood up.

"It's snack time for the kids. Would you girls like some juice and graham crackers?"

"No thank you," we answered. Rose walked away to the kitchenette.

I looked over at Victor, hoping he would speak up. He exchanged glances with his wife, before leaning in to us.

"We haven't told Mama, we think we know what happened," Vic said softly.

"What?!" we whispered, leaning in, almost afraid to hear the answer.

"Well. There's a new prison been under construction several miles out of town, getting built by the company I work for. We'd been wondering about it, you know. Our facility is a little overcrowded but not enough to justify building a whole new prison. And our company was keeping quiet about it. And we had questions, you know? I mean, were they going to send some of us out there when it opened, or hire a new crew for it, or shut down the one we're at?

And finally, just last week, my boss told me I'll be transferring to the new facility, and it's going to house several hundred inmates from another state.And that's unusual. Nobody houses inmates from other states. There's too much interstate red tape to make that worthwhile. They told us inmates were on the way but it would take a while for them to get here. And I was like, where are they coming from, the other side of the country? Turns out, *yeah*. From *Arizona*."

He paused to look at each of us knowingly. I looked around at the others, perplexed.

"I don't get it," Maggie said, shaking her head.

"What I think is happening, is the police are clearing out neighborhoods and shipping the people off to work camps far away from home."

"Holy shit," Shelby breathed. "Sorry."

"And that means there's no telling where our neighbors are. They could be anywhere. But I bet they aren't around here."

"Why would they even do that?" Maggie asked, her face contorted with horror.

"Ain't much good to escape if you don't know where you are," Victor replied. "Got no friends nearby, nobody to help you, no money, no nothing."

"Wow," I sighed.

"But wait, how do you know it's a work camp, and not just a prison?" Shelby asked.

"Honey, most prisons are work camps anymore. Especially the ones run by my company. They specialize in that. We make apparel for department stores. 'Proudly made in the USA' they say on the tags. But it's basically slave labor."

"How can you work in a place like that?" Shelby asked abruptly. Victor looked at her.

"Honey, if there's only two jobs available, I'm gonna take the one on this side of the bars."

"But why are they clearing out whole neighborhoods? These aren't convicted criminals. They're just people," I argued. Grace and Victor shrugged.

"Wait, I remember…." Shelby interjected, wide-eyed. "The luxury condos. The wine bar. They replaced your neighborhood with that."

"What?" Grace said, stunned.

"OH, that makes sense," I said, feeling defeated and angry at the same time. "Get rid of the poor people, replace them with rich ones."

"We'd appreciate it if you didn't tell Mama about this. She's got enough to worry about as it is."

"No, we understand," I assured them. "And we'd better be going anyway. We have medicine to deliver."

"That's right, you have your own to take care of," Grace and Victor said, nodding.

"Hey, are you in touch with anyone else in the area?" Shelby asked.

"Yes, actually. There are a couple more churches in the city that are doing what we're doing, keeping minority families safe and hidden. We trade supplies with each other sometimes. There's another church a couple miles away that I deliver supplies to. But we don't dare talk to our co-workers about what's going on. You can't tell who believes what anymore," Grace added, shaking her head.

"Wow, a real underground!" Maggie sighed, practically with stars in her eyes.

"But it's hard to communicate with them. Our phone service has only gotten worse with time. Seems like we either get a network unavailable message, or get voicemail. We're down to two phones, mine and Grace's, for emergencies. The rest we shut off. We can't afford them anyway."

"Same with our phones," I replied. "We thought it was spotty reception out in the country, but maybe it's just the new normal. But here are our numbers just in case." I sent them to Grace's phone. "We can come back and check on you, see if you need anything."

"Thank you," Vic said to us, shaking our hands. "Grace and I are working, but the others here can't. So we've got to stretch our money just to pay for food."

That got me in the feels, knowing they're trying to feed so many people they barely know. I felt a twinge of regret, not immediately offering our food to help them. But I didn't feel like I should offer anything without my group's consent.

We said our goodbyes and drove home buzzing with the discovery we weren't the only ones underground.

Our news lit a fire under Twinkie. As soon as we told her, she started pacing around the pole barn like a domestic dervish, starting to wipe this clean, then wandering over there, and dusting that, and carrying random items around to set them down for no apparent reason. The dog sensed her excitement and followed her around. I watched them both as Maggie talked excitedly.

"They even said they have an underground network," Maggie described. "Is that not amazing? Like, straight out of a book!" I watched Stephanie roll her eyes a little, but she kept it inconspicuous.

"That is amazing," Twinkie agreed. "And I can't believe I hadn't thought of it before."

"It's not really the sort of thing people advertise," Stephanie said. "You can't really walk around asking people to give up secrets like that."

"But now we know," Twinkie replied, "and that gives me an idea. Actually, three ideas. Are you thirsty?" She bustled out to the water pump, filled our kettle, then set it above the dwindling campfire. We filed outside behind her. Suddenly, she was focused again, stoking the fire with one practiced hand, gesturing for us to sit down around her with the other hand. We obeyed with bated breath.

"Ladies…" she paused, looking at each of us in the eye. "First, let's offer to let our new friends at that church live in Jack's house. I bet they'd like to stretch out. Get some fresh air and sunshine."

"Oh Twinkie, that would be wonderful," Maggie exclaimed. "I was hoping you'd say that."

"Yeah, me too," I said. "It might be tough sneaking them here, but it's doable. They'd be safe here."

Nicole cut in worriedly, "Guys, our garden isn't big enough to support that many people."

"They can take advantage of all this extra land to grow their own food," Twinkie replied.

Stephanie smirked, a twinkle in her eye. "Are you assuming all Hispanic people know how to work a field?"

"No, dumbass, I'm assuming we can teach them if they want to learn." Twinkie grinned back at her.

"They have their own food supply through Grace and Victor, at least until next year," Maggie assured Nicole. "What they need is more space. Their basement was so cramped, and they don't dare show themselves upstairs and risk a raid."

"And what we need is more people," Twinkie added. "We have enough natural resources, we could help a lot more people, but it would take more people to maintain it. And I am definitely ready to start helping more people."

"We'd end up with a nurse on the premises, which would be handy considering how often we injure ourselves out here... *Stephanie....*" I commented pointedly.

"Then all we need is a grave digger, and we'd be set!" Stephanie replied.

An awkward silence broke our conversation.

"We can't tell them about the attack," I said. "They're good people. They'd never agree to come out here if they knew what I did."

"What WE did," said Maggie. "I agree with you. What's done is done, and there's nothing more to talk about."

Silence again, but this time it felt less awkward, more resolute.

"Okay, that's settled…." Twinkie broke the silence. "Second, I think we should start making an effort to join this network, and even expand it. Make it stronger."

"Make it great again?" Stephanie joked.

Twinkie grimaced at her, and waved her fire pokey stick at her melodramatically. "Don't you even!" she said. We all laughed.

"No, I'm serious, just like I was about helping people. It's time to get back into the game. We have something to offer the world, so let's offer it. We'll have a purpose. No more hiding."

Her words took us all aback.

"Guess I never thought about it that way," Shelby said softly.

"I like us helping each other," Nicole added, "But it wouldn't be hard to branch out." Katie, sitting next to her, nodded in agreement.

"Well, I've always wanted to do something like that, be a conductor on the Underground Railroad. I just never thought it would ever happen again."

"Me neither," I agreed.

Steam flew out of the kettle. Just as it began to whistle, Twinkie plucked it from the fire pit and poured its contents into our tea cups stationed on the bench next to her. One by one, she unwrapped and dunked a tea bag into each of our cups; fruity herbal tea for Nicole and Maggie, Oolong for me and Katie, and strong black tea for the rest of us. She always remembers what we want. One by one, she passed the cups around the circle to us.

I broke the silence. "You know, sometimes you read about stories like that, and wonder what you'd do if you lived through that time. Well, now we're living it. And now we have our answer."

"Don't pat yourself on the back just yet," Twinkie replied. "There's a third thing I think we should do."

"What's that?" Shelby asked.

Twinkie took a deep breath and looked around the fire at us slowly.

"Stop hiding and running, and actually do something. Go out and help people. Stop letting this train wreck slowly unfold. Start fighting this system that's screwing us left and right."

"That's a lot of starting and stopping," I remarked.

"Well yeah, nobody just picks a heroic challenge and sails through it."

"That's true. So what are you suggesting?" I asked.

"I mean get into the fray. They make a thing, we tear it down. Like the prison." Twinkie handed me a tea bag.

"That's crazy. There's no way we can do something like that."

"Yeah we can," she asserted confidently, blowing the steam off her tea.

"You're out of your mind."

"It's just a building. And that building is full of people on our side who want to get out. And we have someone on the inside ready to help us - Victor."

"That's a good point." I looked away to think for a minute. "But we don't know how to break people out of a prison."

"Neither do I, but we can figure out how."

"It probably involves kicking someone's ass, and I'm still disappointed I missed my last chance," Stephanie commented.

We dunked our tea bags for a minute in silence.

"You're serious?" Shelby asked Twinkie.

"Yeah, I am."

I opened my mouth to give some reasons why we shouldn't try, but couldn't think of any.

"How *could* we possibly pull off a stunt like that?" Stephanie asked, intrigued in spite of herself.

Twinkie countered our skepticism with the grin I've always loved.

"Don't worry. I have a plan."

THE END

www.ingramcontent.com/pod-product-compliance
Lightning Source LLC
Chambersburg PA
CBHW031706170626
46808CB00005B/1635